G000091303

About the Author

From preparatory school to graduation day she always doubted the suitability of her education for a career in offshore engineering. Apparently morning meetings on North Sea platforms are not conducted in Middle English. Never once was her opinion sought on the aftermath of the Peloponnesian wars.

She was, however, frequently asked: "Can you type?"

Eventually, she rose to head up her own department in an international offshore contracting company.

Many years a full-time mother followed, and has concluded.

Creativity, and a new challenge, were sought and found in writing. Thus the twenty short stories comprising *The Shortbread Tales* came to fruition.

Mrs Milligan

THE SHORTBREAD TALES

AUSTIN MACAULEY PUBLISHERS™

LONDON • CAMBRIDGE • NEW YORK • SHARJAH

A CIP catalogue record for this title is available from the British Library.

ISBN 9781528998826 (Paperback)
ISBN 9781528998833 (Hardback)
ISBN 9781528998840 (ePub e-book)

www.austinmacauley.com

First Published (2020)
Austin Macauley Publishers Ltd
25 Canada Square
Canary Wharf
London
E14 5LQ

Acknowledgements

From these I have read and learned:
To: P.G. Wodehouse, for his outrageous sense of fun, and incomparable use of adjectives.
To: Somerset Maugham, for his consummate skill as a master raconteur.
To: Jeffrey Archer, for continuing the tradition of first rate short stories.

The story 'Per Ardua ad Astra' references "Growltiger's Last Stand" from *Old Possum's Book of Practical Cats* by T.S. Eliot. It appears by kind permission of Faber and Faber.

'The Dragons of Bethenhurst' tale is indebted to the unknown author of the poem 'Memories'.

Contents

Part 1

The Elixir of Life

Incarcerated as I was for five years in the hitherto unexplored heathland and forest of Southeast England, I was exiled from my native Scotland to preparatory school at the princely age of 8. Here I was to discover, at the leisurely pace necessary to while away the years until the all-important Common Entrance exams, what it is like as a boarder at a very English prep school, from a boy's perspective.

My first question, directed to my house-parent, was, "Is there a time difference in this country?"

I was abruptly reminded that the question should be re-phrased thus: "Sir, is there a time difference in this country?"

An only child, used to my own space and constantly being viewed by my mother as a 'rather special little person' (R.S.L.P.). I was cast as a front-runner for the Eton Entry Stakes; frankly, I had a better chance at winning the 2,000 Guineas than achieving a place at this hallowed institution. My appearance at the entrance test was perhaps not helped by my managing to slam the door firmly shut in the face of the then Headmaster of the said college on entrance test day.

The test result that followed seemed inevitable.

Previously, I had frequently been warned by my mother when sighting tramps on city street corners bedding down for the night, 'that is what happens if you do not pass the Common Entrance!' This was used as a form of encouragement to do well at school.

My poor mother was destined for disappointment right from the start. I decided from the onset that throughout a sustained period of truly diabolical food, of draughty shared dorms and seemingly endless events where prowess at singing seemed to be the only real quality needed to succeed in life, I was probably better suited to having fun at home.

When the headmaster's wife had asked me when I looked around the school, "Are you looking forward to joining us?"

My reply, "No, I'd rather be at home with Mummy," had become prophetic.

The main focus was to be trying my hand at every opportunity that came my way. Rugby to pottery, the clarinet to polo, were already firmly in my sights. With no elder sibling to forewarn me of the life ahead, I began to feel like one of the numerous foreign pupils whose parents had been attracted to the British prep school system for reasons that still remain a mystery to me. My thought process was based on 'get good at something and you will gain friends'.

Unfortunately for me, everyone else had a similar strategic plan and I had no contingency should this not work.

The net result was competition—something I had not encountered before. This seemed endemic in the entire system. To my mind, everyone seemed pretty good at academic work and I was unable to establish sufficient prowess at virtually anything. So, I became the joker of the class, and did no work. I was not particularly good at any team sport, which I rarely took seriously. I very soon tanked in term one. Finally, determined to survive, I decided to observe my fellow creatures with a critical eye, be it staff or pupils, and take a 'tongue in cheek' glance at prep school life; here I thought I had found my forte.

There was a fascinating range of potential material to hand. I was not slow to grasp the comic and quirky behaviour of my comrades and, more especially, their parents. The latter ranged from heads of corporate finance (daughter obviously head-girl-in-waiting) to those beleaguered and impoverished enslaving themselves to three sets of public school fees, plus vast cash-devouring derelict and once grand mansion homes.

My first exeat weekend was an eye-opener on several accounts. A succession of apprehensive parents drove at a stately pace up the long drive to the imposing main school building. As usual, in these situations, the 'imposing main building' is exclusively used for the headmaster's study, the library where a log fire glows in the grate, and a couple of administrative kennels. The only other usage known to man is to feature prominently in the photography of the school prospectus.

Pupils enter at their peril!

Parents emanated from vehicles as diverse as the collectable maroon Morris Minor Traveller to the stockbroker sleek Aston Martin. Most contained an assortment of canine travellers. They arrived at the library to sign out their offspring.

I was looking forward to the arrival of my currently unknown escort and to escape Downlands for a complete day and a half! What exciting vehicle would swish towards the portico to deliver me to a weekend of luxury and homeliness? To include a lie-in (compulsory) and a cosy comfortable kitchen laden with Aga-cooked food and surrounded by spaniels (optional). A room of my own and above all, an escape from ringing school bells for thirty-six hours or more. It all sounded so unbearably good… As my thoughts escalated along these lines until I could virtually smell the beef roasting on Sunday morning as I tiptoed across the thick pile of my bedroom carpet, only to discover my dream shattered.

A 'Cherry Picker' crane was the only vehicle left in the carpark and the parental owner was advancing towards the library with open arms to welcome back into the family fold my friend, with whom I was destined to spend the weekend.

Astutely, I realised at once that mentioning this odd mode of transport was not a topic to feature in my opening gambit. I therefore determined only to mention the vehicle when my host felt it appropriate. No one ever mentioned the unorthodox mode of travel via crane.

As we rumbled through the countryside, with a minor armada of vehicles to the rear, we eventually turned off into a private road perforated with more potholes than Cheddar Gorge. The jib was bouncing dramatically at every new lump and bump. This slow procession was conducted largely in silence (due to engine noise) and seemed never-ending. As the light was beginning to fade on this chilly November afternoon, my ears were tingling with the cold. I winced as we squeezed the outsized vehicle over a tiny humped back bridge.

I could just discern a vast and rambling stone-built structure coming into view in the gloaming. I felt like Rommel partly protruding from his tank as we advanced towards this fortress. Arriving in the courtyard, one could see the outline of a once fine Georgian building that looked, and proved to be, virtually uninhabitable. Beneath the vast stone pillars at the entrance—Ozymandias would have been proud of them—were several bulging Iceland bags, presumably containing our supplies for the weekend, which had been worryingly abandoned.

Andrew went cheerfully into the hall, by now in near total darkness, and clicked on the light switch. Nothing happened.

"Off the electric, I suppose, again," he commented cheerfully while pulling on a pair of rubber boots to go inside. I watched this operation as Andrew donned the rest of his protective clothing to enter his home.

"I'd put on a pair of wellies if I were you," he suggested. "The house is pretty damp in parts," he added with sincerity, showing a continued concern for my well-being.

"Those are the visitors' boots; they are mostly in pairs," he added. Eventually, I found one black and one green welly boot; both were an approximate and acceptable fit for the left foot. These were mandatory kit for the long journey down the darkened corridor.

My first adventure along this corridor in near black-out conditions was very well musically orchestrated and rather memorable. The entire length of the dingy passage was, I discovered, lined with dogs' beds. I stumbled along as my eyes were beginning to get used to the lack of light. I tripped over, and into, each bed in turn, whereupon the disgruntled occupant yowled indignantly and promptly bit me. This unpleasant experience was repeated innumerable times before Andrew threw open a huge double wooden door and said: "This is the dining room. In a bit of a mess, I'm afraid."

This was an understatement as the entire roof had fallen in apparently some time ago—the dining table and floor were strewn with rubble and masonry. As a point of edification,

Andrew added: "We didn't clear the table, it didn't seem worth it really—anyway, Vogue Japan did a fashion shoot in here shortly afterwards." The food indeed was still in evidence on the table, everything remained untouched.

As we trudged diligently onwards along the ground floor, my initial excitement for my first exeat weekend was replaced by a feeling probably only truly really experienced by a routed and retreating army. Indeed, I began to feel great empathy towards the few remaining Napoleonic troops leaving Russia in total disarray and defeat in 1812.

Entering the kitchen, a tall blonde woman—naturally clad in wellington boots—said, "Welcome to the only room in the house with any heating." She thereupon pointed towards an antiquated Belling cooker, which was sited next to, and dwarfed by, a grand piano. She sat down and without a word began to play. A flurry of dogs left the room post-haste.

The prospect of tea seemed faint; given our hostess, who had attended Oxford, was now engrossed in a lengthy concerto on the piano. Andrew shouted, "Fancy an ice-cream?" opening the lid of a large chest freezer. I peered in to review the choice hoping a favourite, Raspberry Ripple, would feature on the menu. Alas, no such luck.

I pulled back and gasped. There, lying in the deep freezer completely intact, was a Jack Russell terrier. Stiff and covered in frost. This time, I felt bound to comment.

Andrew airily replied that it had been run over on the road outside the estate and his father had frozen it in case the owner wanted the body back. He then added that they usually have a few road kills in the freezer anyway and some of them end up on the barbeque. I was about to enquire if they had any plan for a barbeque this weekend and decided against it! I completely forgot about the ice-cream. However, my thoughts at this point did turn a little hesitantly towards dinner…

The weekend progressed with Andrew, also aged eight, taking me for drives in his ancient Mini Cooper car (floor completely absent) around the estate. A short interlude where we all pursued deer poachers on the land with guns. Finally, an organ recital held in the music room, where the seating arrangements for the audience were airline seats bought from obsolete aircraft, complete with safety harnesses! All this was conducted in a property with all the modern convenience and comfort of a transit camp.

Andrew subsequently wrote and published a book in his first year of public school aged thirteen. He did not attend university and is currently employed as a professional author.

My next home visit was equally bizarre and memorable for a variety of reasons. This time, the backcloth of a sprawling mock Tudor mansion, complete with tennis court, Italianate gardens and a swimming pool, was somewhat marred by the fact this enormous house had been barely cleaned this century. Apparently, a succession of nannies and cleaners had fled the establishment on arrival and had subsequently been treated for shock. None had left any mark or stamp of hygiene before they departed. There was a permanent smell of escaping gas pervading the entire premises. This compound when inhaled with the constant presence of cat litter trays (yes, you guessed it, rarely emptied) gave the place an odour foxes strived to emulate to ward off zealous hounds.

This was the home of two well-respected intellectuals, both holding senior medical positions within the profession. Their four scruffy protégés had all attended Downlands and Oxbridge thereafter. Rupert, my classmate, was lucky enough to be able to choose between scholarships—classics, science, music and art were all well within his reach.

Food and drink were undoubtedly the passion in this household. It would be difficult to overemphasise the seriousness with which both of these Epicurean delights were upheld.

Adjacent to the kitchen was a culinary library, with cookery tomes stacked literally from floor to ceiling. I had high expectations of the delights in store at the family Sunday lunch, and I was not to be disappointed.

Lunch lasted from approximately one to six pm and consisted of countless adequate courses, with time enough between them to stimulate the appetite to accept just a little more!

This was followed, shortly afterwards, by school boys' delight—afternoon tea—sadly, surgeon and father Richard was called away from the lunch table where he had assiduously been absorbing a volume on surgery for breast reductions between courses. Just before main course was carved, a private patient called at the house, who held an appointment with Richard to remove some stitches. Casting aside his knife, fork and book, he attended.

Somewhat unfortunately, Richard's wife, our hostess, informed us she had just run the poor chap over outside the house. Unfazed by the fact, she had reversed into the patient, thereby pinning him to the exterior wall of the dining room, she slipped away from producing any further food and beverage to take him to her hospital where she treated the poor fellow for broken ribs and other minor injuries.

We helped ourselves to pudding.

Luckily, she was back in time to produce afternoon tea-time-tasties, before returning us to school. At least this interlude limited her fond recollections and non-stop flow of reminiscences of her favourite autopsies. These included the measurement and weight in grams of the livers of various celebrities and pop stars. Later, I was to be treated to a week of their lavish hospitality at their Italian villa.

Rupert successfully undertook a scholarship and thereafter found his 'spiritual home' following in his family footsteps at Cambridge.

After matches, be it home or away, was often an ideal way to meet parents and mingle amongst their most definitely preferable assortment of tea goodies. It always was a fascination to me how those that actually played and entertained via the match received a Kit Kat and a cordial drink, whilst the supporters were delicately served a buffet that would not be out of place at Fortnum's. The injustice of it all…

One could also view visiting siblings—both older and younger—and appraise potential new starts at Downlands.

On one notable occasion, a Bulgarian father turned up on a muddy rugby pitch wearing a white wool three-piece suit, large felt hat and sporting a black city-style umbrella (he was noticeable mainly for his lack of Barbour and wellies). He remained stoic throughout underneath his umbrella in the damp conditions. He later marched off to the Junior Boys' changing rooms to rendezvous with his son. Walking through the rooms in his unusual attire raised a few wary eyebrows amongst the boys. Solemnly, he lowered his black umbrella, shaking off the residual drops on the floor, and bellowed at the assembled multitude in a strong Bulgarian accent: "Bite me!"

The apparition then left without a further word. His son also disappeared from school in a similarly abrupt fashion.

Tea completed, the fond farewells in the carpark came next; these were marked by the transfer of fodder from four-wheel drive vehicles into strategic bushes, from whence these delectables would be retrieved at a later date and consumed with consummate passion.

Here also, one held gem-like conversations with a variety of parents. These gave fascinating insights into the lives of fellow pupils.

One lean and leggy blonde determined to wear high heels throughout the football season was invariably found welded into the pitch, heels down, trapped by her own footwear. She could be heard wailing behind the ha-ha long after play had ceased and well into early evening.

On rescuing her at the onset of darkness from her predicament, we chatted about holidays on the return to civilisation, namely the Junior Boys common room. Whereupon she confided in me that despite having taken her tribe of five on a fortnight's driving tour, covering the ancient churches of Italy and at the hottest time of the year, none of them had actually seemed to enjoy this edifying ecclesiastical experience, to her evident surprise. She turned to me in a genuine quandary. Suppressing a smile, I asked innocently: "Surely Charlie enjoyed the holiday—after all, he is nearly eighteen months old now?" Her deadly serious rejoinder was: "Truly he was the only one who seemed quite content."

I surmised that he must have very wisely slept throughout most of the trip!

Bidding her farewell and Amen, I waved as the customary regal procession of Range Rovers headed down the drive, each sporting a brace or more of canines peering desperately out of steamy rear-view windows.

On another less startling occasion, a doctor of physics arrived on a Sunday morning in late October to take his son to lunch at home in Sussex. I greeted the familiar face with a smile and said: "Gosh! I am surprised to see you here, Doctor Wood." He returned the friendly smile, which quickly disappeared as a wave of realisation swept across his face.

"Oh my God," he said, "I'm at the wrong school, George is at Eton now, I had forgotten." He had to dash up the motorway without delay to complete the one-and-a-half-hour trip to the right school. George had left Downlands in June, nearly four months ago! I wondered if the dizzy doctor had even noticed. I pondered; perhaps this change would register when he glanced at the heading on the end of term bill.

Walking across the hallway, I noticed, marooned on a large sofa, the headmaster seated outside his study. He was marking a pile of exercise books. His knees clamped together, thus preventing the terracotta coloured books falling between his thin legs. His lanky body was bent to his task. Isolated from his usual habitat, the head's study, he sighed sadly in his banishment. He looked up in answer to my unspoken question and explained: "I'm here as young Prendergast has taken delivery of an antique harp of great value. His parents have assured me that my study is the only place suitable and large enough to house the precious object." Finally, he added: "I am sure he will complete his music practice shortly and I will be able to return to my study." He paused. "Heavenly," he concluded appreciatively, closing his eyes at the near perfect playing from the room next door.

Not stopping to reply, I continued ascending the staircase. I paused as my eye was caught by the spectacle of young Prendergast perched behind the headmaster's desk savouring his new surroundings. He sat facing towards his harp, which was positioned on the opposite side of the room. Suddenly, he leant forward, delved into his jacket pocket and produced with theatrical flourish a giant Mars bar! Eagerly devouring his cache, he nonchalantly dropped the wrapper to the floor to join the others in the pile below him. All the while he was listening to a tape of Welsh harp music!

It's always pleasantly reassuring to find the quality of consistency in any organisation. As I climbed the next flight of stairs, I reflected on this and my thoughts wandered. Here I was for five years immersed in the countryside singing, playing sport, carefully tackling the complexities of Greek and Latin grammar with a complement of staff, children and occasionally parents that were by and large gifted, talented and…well, hardly mainstream.

Gradually, enlightenment was beginning to dawn on me. A realisation what life boarding at a very English prep school was all about. Eureka! Had I put my finger on it and distilled the essence of prep school life?

There was an oddball charm to the whole activity, and the common denominator had to be a mild, yet consistent craziness throughout. From top to bottom.

Suddenly, it all made sense…or did it? Anyway, I concluded, if this was consistency it was fun. And fun was what I wanted. I had another four years before me to work out the finer details of how this enduring English system of education has stood the test of time and, not only survived, but met with such unrivalled success.

Tiger Balm

A Catholic in a Muslim country, brought up by Iban tribesmen in a longhouse, and educated by nuns. A former soldier with the Malay SAS, and currently a jungle guide. A man of surprising contrasts. By any standards, he had experienced a despicable day. Even his bush hat looked dishevelled, as he sat alone brooding. Hit by loose logs floating downstream, our craft had capsized catapulting our small party into the violent river. He had managed the emergency expertly.

Now he stared morosely at the solid grey curtain of rain; a silent witness contemplating the events of the day. He didn't drink, so I bought him a stiff gin. We talked.

His dream was to travel to Great Britain. Based on his voracious reading of the adventures of "The Famous Five". He had read them all.

I hated to disillusion him—Britain had changed since the days of Aunt Fanny and Uncle Quentin. I began to feel a maternal protection towards this man: so capable in his own world, but potentially so lost in modern British society.

Finally, I persuaded him to stay at my house and to accept my hospitality during his trip to Britain, it would be a pleasure to look after him. Agreement was reached. Conversation ceased.

"What did you do when you left the SAS?" I enquired.

"Palm oil plantation security, intercepting Filipino pirate raids," he replied.

Then he added, with the complete candour of a child:

"I shot them all—there were 18 in total."

Après-ski

"The quiet side of the mountain", proclaimed the holiday advert. Just what I was seeking for an aspiring 7-year-old skier. No noisy nightlife or après-ski. Just encouraging rather than challenging slopes, a warm traditional alpine hotel complete with log fire and a fitness centre. The scenic beauty of Lake Pertisau may prove less vital for the little one, but safe skiing, a short transfer and plenty of wiener schnitzel would be 'just the job'. Sure to keep both of us happy for a week after Christmas and before the new term began.

After an invigorating day on the snow-covered mountains, we were ready to follow up with a sortie to discover the leisure facilities, which were shared with the adjacent hotel. The delights of the Turkish baths, gym and swimming pool, I hoped awaited us.

Realistically, I was fully expecting to see a familiar and unwelcoming notice pinned to the health suite's door in the vein of 'CHILDREN UNDER 10 YEARS OF AGE ARE PROHIBITED FROM USING THESE FACILITIES'.

I was both relieved and pleasantly surprised to find no such notice.

At this point, the hotel was less than half full, and a passing friendship was developing between my son and I and the couple who nightly dined at the table next to ours.

She was, I would say, 40-42 years of age, with a long neck, straight back and the carriage of one trained as a classical dancer. Yet she was too tall for an ex-ballerina. Her long slim physique was crowned with shoulder-length strawberry blonde hair. This combined with her flawless skin gave her a youthful carefree look. Clearly, her life had not been dogged by worry or misfortune, as there were no tell-tale lines on her angelic face.

I thought she would make a marvellous artist's model as the Madonna in a religious artwork.

He, in direct physical contrast, was about 60, short, extremely rotund and wore thick glasses. A miniature Buddha. I concluded that, had I been a producer type-casting for a play requiring a country vicar, he, without doubt, would be my choice.

My analysis proved prophetic, as closer encounters with the pair revealed that he was a professor of divinity at a particularly renowned Scottish university. She also worked in academia. They were not married.

The pair proved to be good company and well-travelled. As far as I knew, we were the only four Brits in the hotel, and having discovered we all lived in Scotland, our little chats developed a pace.

Early one evening, my son and I decided to take to the Turkish bath. As I entered the steam-filled marble-clad mausoleum, I noticed everyone had removed their clothes and were merely sitting on their towels, which I had taken to be modesty wear.

Naturally, Jack and I followed the regime and sat around the edge of the central marble plinth with our towels on the wet marble beneath our botties.

Despite the dense mist and steam, I could just discern our dining companions seated opposite to us, she waved a friendly greeting towards us. He remained still as, despite the fact he was wearing his glasses, he could see little in the fog. I imagined, possibly with closed eyes he was in contemplation of higher things: ecclesiastical conundrums eschatology or maybe merely considering the prospects on this evening's menu... Who is to tell?

As his head bent forward, nodding a little as he did so, I felt he could just be about to drop off to sleep.

Jack, my son, had now sat still for going on five minutes before he remarked: "Mummy, none of these people have any clothes on!"

His powers of observation have always been notable.

No reply was forthcoming from me as I felt he had assessed the situation succinctly. Nothing of use could be added.

Immediately, I realised he had reached his threshold of tolerance with regard to sitting still and doing nothing. It was at that point he got up and peered more closely at a few random guests, presumably just to check their gender, and moved on.

Under the marble bench seat upon which the bathers were ensconced was a large plastic-coated hose. Blue in colour. Jack picked the hose up from the floor and looked down the wide bore of the tool.

"What does that do, Mummy?"

"Well, I think it might be for hosing down the facility after it has closed. To clean up," I said lazily.

The damp heat of the Turkish bath was beginning to dull my brain, which should have detected a warning at this point—"boys and water don't mix" or is it oil and water?

I sat back sleepily to close my eyes and relax, while he pottered.

Unbeknown to me and undetected in the growing fog of the bath, he was obviously following the length of the hose to its source. Evidently, a large metal tap wheel was attached to the wall beneath our marble seats, not unlike the ones used to allow water through lock gates. To his mind, this intriguing combination of water and mechanics was totally irresistible. The opportunity this discovery afforded was unmissable. He turned the tap slightly, just to see if it worked. Nothing happened.

Holding the pipe in his hand, he focussed on the diameter, not a drop of water came out. Perplexed, he scrabbled about on the floor again heading straight for the tap. I mumbled: "Jack, stop fidgeting and sit down," only to be heard by deaf ears.

Meanwhile, under the bench a clonking sound, often associated with trapped water within a pipe, was faintly audible. Jack was still on his hands and knees and he began to stand up with the plastic tube under his arm and pointing backwards into the room.

There was a single hideous screech.

This came from the occupant of the marble seat directly opposite the open end of the hose pipe.

As I opened my eyes, I witnessed a torrent of ice-cold water shooting through the air with the ferocity of a fire hydrant tackling a tall building ablaze.

It had struck our theologian. A direct hit in his private parts.

Holding himself tightly across this devastated area, he bolted across the room "in extremis"; he was closely followed by his partner whose "countenance divine" was contorted with concern. It must have been a brief but memorable experience.

The hose was turned off, calm restored to our former haven of relaxation and Jack said: "Do you think I should say sorry, Mummy?"

On reflection, I felt his timing on this one wasn't too good. So I replied, "No!" which obviously surprised him.

Before I went down to the bar that evening, I felt it might be wise to have a word with the maître d'hôtel, to ask if perhaps we could have another table on this occasion. A little further away from our friends.

This apparently could not be accommodated. I began to consider the prospects of eating out, but discarded this as a cowardly response, and anyway the food was awfully good in.

Crossing the hotel foyer, heading for the lift, I glimpsed Jack's unwitting victim as he limped slowly towards the dining room.

Relations with the next door table that evening were difficult to describe. Controlled is possibly the most positive adjective I can come up with. The injured party's partner managed a few frosty exchanges. However, he remained silent throughout the meal. Jack looked sheepish and rather down-hearted, until our former friend did speak.

Then we all looked a little shame-faced. He opened his mouth and squeaked.

He spoke in a high-pitched voice, not regularly associated with a full-grown man, perhaps more suited to choir boys.

Confronting his students at his next lecture might need an explanation to account for his delivery in this new higher vocal note. Several ideas came to mind.

A freak skiing accident?

Could it be attributed to some biblical revelation or experience? A miracle perhaps?

Or would he come clean and admit it was a 7-year-old with a plastic water hose that had caused the transformation!

He didn't actually ask for my advice, so, given the circumstances, I didn't offer any!

The Laird

Stag horn blown, the beaters lined out in horseshoe shape seem to rise from the heather as one. They advance with military precision, slowly moving forward, carefully orchestrated by keepers with walkie-talkies in contact with their counterparts behind the butts.

Battle plan in place. They halt part of the line briefly to prevent birds leaking out at the sides of the bowl shape. Then forward; flags unfurling in the autumn breeze.

I live for the grouse season. Let me tell you why. The sights, sounds and smells of the day are the epitome of pleasure for me—not the bag.

You could leave behind the modern world, completely. Rolling heather-clad hills, the occasional moss hag, a scattering of burns and the odd bothy, there is nothing to remind you of this century. Unchanging from season to season: Scotland at its best, and not a tourist in sight.

Magic, pure magic.

All the vital ingredients and the order of battle remain both timeless and perfect; I would not change it for the world. A handful of strategically placed stone butts on the ridge form a defensive wall and are occupied by the family and invited guests. Earlier, loaders had decanted an assortment of hand-made gun cases there ready for action. My favourite is the zebra skin set.

Visible clouds of pollen waft into the air as Labradors, belonging to the pickers-up, begin to thrash about expectantly in the heather. Tension builds as keepers, under-keepers, stalkers, gillies and estate workers are drafted into service on shooting days in August and September. These troops all know the lie of the land. Resplendent, they wear plus twos and jackets in the estate tweed. Like uniform, their dress imposes a sense of order, a discipline, upon the operation. Flashings in their shooting stockings are details carefully designed for practicality and to impress. So similar to military strategy.

I am like a General reviewing the rank and file.

Ah! There go the wicker hampers—one, two, three—rations that I trust will include our raised game pie; one of the tantalising specialities of the house. Not forgetting the traditional grouse season tipple: homemade sloe gin. Moderation with the latter or the guests won't be able to manage fishing the trout loch further down the valley this evening. Of course, they may opt for the duck-flighting, depending on what time the last game drive ends.

Best to check whether the fire is lit at the lodge, and the seating plan at the table, so all is in hand for lunchtime. We always put on a good show; so no harm in checking the details…

A covey of birds is dislodged by the line. They explode into the air. Subsequently, a barrage of smells excite my nostrils, as the sound of lead shot whistles directly overhead. Gunpowder, waxed jackets, hot gun oil. The powerful horsey smell of the little red-brown birds themselves. All this enveloped in the soft scent of heather in flower. Truly, the sense of smell is one of life's greatest pleasures.

Meanwhile, damp spaniels, in search of grounded birds, lunge into the bracken to the accompanying sound of gun dog whistles and commands of 'Hi Loss, Hi Loss'!

Shot grouse are housed in hessian sacks until the end of the pre-lunch drive. The sacks have a special aroma all of their own. Now, at mid-day, the birds will be counted and transferred to the game cart, where they are hung in pairs. Later to be stored in the game larder.

I hear the 100 yard whistle, no more shots can be taken. The drive is at an end.

Well, best foot forward. If I remain seated in this Land Rover any longer, I will be stiff and slow. Time to welcome them back and enquire about their morning's sport.

So, with a regal swish of my tail and a nuzzle up against their shooting stockings, I will acknowledge my guests and make my presence felt at the lodge.

Three Maroon Cherries

One-armed bandits and fruit machines had hitherto proved my only occasional brush with technology. This was until the advent of the Automatic Teller Machine (ATM). These new-fangled 'holes in the wall' seemed to possess magical qualities: they could be consulted like oracles and relied upon to dispense cash—even at the most bewitching hours. They provided a lifeline to impoverished undergraduates, enabling the small pot of cash necessary to cover the meagre needs of a student, to be rifled seven days of the week!

To my adolescent mind, ATMs were akin to fruit machines displaying three maroon cherries in a row, and consistently yielding a cash prize as a result!

It was early on a cheerless Sunday morning; a grey unforgiving sky lay over the Northern town. The rain lashed down and this was accompanied by a flesh-tearing wind. It was too early to hear the usual Salvation Army Band parade. The shipyard lay idle.

As a first-year student, dressed in a purple Lycra exercise suit en route to an aerobics class, I stopped at the local bank. One man stood in front of the ATM, addressing the screen in the position of a golfer preparing to tee off. Bending down cautiously, he produced his plastic card and, pushing it into the slot, waited.

There was no encouraging gurgle or response from the machine. Just silence. He waited. Still nothing.

He tapped the machine in an exasperated attempt at persuasion that didn't pay off. Then waited.

Snatching his card, he turned on his heel to face the driving rain. He pulled up the collar of his donkey jacket as he braced himself before walking fully into wind. Shoulders up and head down, his face was obscured as he dissolved into the grey abyss.

I moved forward to become the next victim.

I began fumbling in pocket after pocket to retrieve my card. No luck! No luck at all. I simply could not find it.

It was then I heard a rickety clattering sound coming from deep within the machine. It appeared to be experiencing some type of painful motion as if it was about to give birth.

To my consternation, it began to disgorge cash, and lots of it! All too soon, the snapping shut of the cash slot was audible and the extraordinary incident was drawn abruptly to a close. I snatched the great wad of notes. Pocketed it and ran off down the street.

Leaping swiftly into action without thought, I was sure I would find my quarry with ease. He could not have gone far. Besides, there was nobody around at this hour and in such foul weather. I turned the corner, save for a few derelict dustbins, the street lay empty.

Bewildered, I looked right and left. I crossed a small carpark. It was then I glimpsed a retreating figure, hands deeply buried in the pockets of a donkey jacket, the collar of which was turned up against the weather. The figure was striding away from me and heading towards the North Sea.

I dashed up to him and tapped him on the shoulder. He stopped and turned directly towards me. The rain was dripping steadily down his face and off his chin. Vacantly, he stared at the rain-soaked apparition, clad in purple Lycra, standing before him.

'Here is your money!' I gasped, thrusting it into his hand before the near gale-force wind ripped it away. In an instant, and without a word, he grabbed the cash and was gone.

I walked slowly back, reflecting that my speedy enthusiastic response had secured one good deed for the day!

Excellent!

Surely?

Luck often comes in disguise, it is true, but it is the recognition of that luck that counts.

I was now beginning to experience a nagging sense of unease, 'job not quite right somehow'.

It was the expression on the stranger's face: such profound incredulity that haunted me. A numb realisation crept over my body making me shiver. Could I really have given a vast wad of cash to a random passer-by?

I peered unseeingly into the empty distance, as the rain bounced off the pavement and splashed up to my knees. An absurd drenched figure. I remained motionless, letting the full import of the moment take root.

In my mind's eye, all I could see was a machine displaying a row of three maroon cherries. This was accompanied by the ringing sound of winning coins rattling and tumbling, but not into a scoop below, a bonanza for me to collect.

These coins were falling, endlessly, through my fingers and seeping out wasted into the depths of the troubled North Sea.

Home Sweet Home

Every inch breathed opulence.
Every foot exuded glamour.
Every acre cried out prestige.
This was no ordinary hotel.

Nestled high on the cliff face, shimmering down on the cove beneath, the hotel stood bathed in sunlight. Verdant greenery sprouted all around to protect the privacy of those privileged to be contained within. This exclusive hideaway was well camouflaged from the prying eyes of the paparazzi. If you were booked into this hotel, you had truly "arrived".

The hotel lobby swished expensively. It had an air of restrained elegance. Immaculately presented bellboys stood poised and ready for action, should any stray item of Louis Vuitton luggage require up lifting. The concierge, half hidden behind a gilt-encrusted antique piece—never to be called a desk—was in attendance and bristling with efficiency.

Brass shone at every angle. The art deco black and white marble floor sparkled. Carefully nurtured potted plants, doubtless placed with precision, were dotted around the entrance hall. They seemed to underline the understated yet orchestrated aura of success and wealth.

Thus, the hotel was singled-out as an establishment not to be trifled with.

Sitting alone, isolated in a corner, was a lady I would guess to be in her early seventies. Slim and pale-faced, she perched on the edge of her enormous chair, hugging her handbag like a three-year-old about to be parted from a beloved teddy bear. She wore pale blue courtelle slacks and a hand-knitted white summer cardi. Complete with opaque buttons the colour of Fox's glacier mints. An immediately recognisable British wardrobe.

She gazed uneasily at her surroundings.

Her white permed hair cast a bizarre shadow on the wall behind her.

She looked like the proverbial 'fish out of water'.

I took a seat opposite her chair and smiled reassuringly. Her opening gambit, somewhat unsurprisingly given the British preoccupation with the subject, was 'the weather'. After a few pleasantries, having noted her Yorkshire accent, I enquired where she came from (meaning which part of God's own country); she gazed reverentially towards heaven, her eyes closed, her thoughts obviously turning to home. It was as if she had entered a private world. Clearly, she was savouring every second of her reverie. She did not speak.

I felt unable to invade her moment of ecstasy by repeating my as yet unanswered question.

I waited, mentally dallying with personal memories of times spent in the great county: the moors, the coastal towns and villages, Helmsley, Staithes, Runswick Bay…

Suddenly, she focussed on me like a bird of prey about to pounce. Yet still she retained that disconcerting and detached look of indulgent pleasure, which emanated from every aspect of her features as she contemplated home.

In an instant, she replied: "Sheffield."

We sat together a little longer, with no words exchanged. The silence was not uncomfortable: I sensed she needed a listening ear.

As she leant forward from the immense chair that engulfed her, I was able to look fully and searchingly into her face. Her mood had changed. Intuition told me her northern stability and levelheadedness were about to give in.

Was she going to let me into her confidence? Unburden herself in some way, as one sometimes does with a complete stranger?

My patience was about to be rewarded as she cast her eyes down and began intriguingly: "I will never do it again."

I raised my eyebrows expectantly, but said nothing.

"It changes everything," she lamented, shaking her head sadly. "The lottery, that's the problem. Winning the lottery."

The Demise of Dennis

Dennis was of quiet demeanour.

Dennis was diffident.

Dennis was, as I was later to discover, extremely devious.

Each morning, as soon as the curtain was drawn, Dennis would appear. My regular breakfast partner, Dennis, was the ideal houseguest: always out of doors invariably on time for meals, and eagerly enjoying everything on offer. No dietary fads entered his savvy head.

Dennis was my darling, a regular visitor who was endlessly grateful for shelter, sustenance and living space. He would frequently appear on the garden wall, where he would commence a type of war dance, which was quite peculiar to him. This involved slowly revolving in a tight circular motion accompanied by a rather agitated bout of wing flapping. There appeared no direct activator for this occasional spontaneous display, performed for my benefit I fondly supposed. Impromptu and on the spur of the moment.

Dennis never disappointed. He was always there every morning, regular as clockwork, hungry, keen and modestly dressed in his grey brown attire. His broad chest, long legs and slender beak gave him a dashing figure amongst the varied garden dwellers.

This imposing form must have been responsible for many sleepless nights in the spider community, to whom Dennis must have been seen as a demon.

Dining on a mix of sunflower seeds and linseed, Dennis was suddenly interrupted by the arrival of a 'giant' on his patch. A male blackbird landing on the flat top of the wall, like a fighter jet on an aircraft carrier. Dennis wobbled violently, as with an equal mix of shock and horror, he realised this monster was about to deprive him of his very next meal! Action was definitely required to restore the balance of power.

Momentarily flummoxed by the audacity of the intruder, Dennis appeared to concede without any resistance or drama and dropped downwards onto the terrace below. Frankly, I was dismayed at his acquiescence and lack of defence of both his meal and his territory.

However, all was not lost.

From his vantage point beneath the enemy, Dennis was able to devise a strategy—a plan of attack upon the marauding freebooter above.

Military tactics and advanced strategic planning were aspects of Dennis' capabilities I had not been privy to prior to this event. True to form, Dennis did not disappoint. From his disadvantaged position, Dennis was able to mount an uphill attack. A daring raid on his assailant; the entire plan was hatched in Dennis's amazing bird-sized brain.

Observing the enemy consuming his delicious nutrients, Dennis flew, wings stretched to the maximum and feathers ruffled to give the illusion of added size, he began to move upwards to face the enemy. A single swift movement later, a full frontal attack was launched. Dennis flew straight into the flank of the blackbird above, striking with his beak one purposeful and profound blow. His full body weight was behind the assault. The net result of the attack was evident immediately. Dennis ricocheted off the impostor in no uncertain terms. No graceful parabola was witnessed; the attacker was observed falling backwards onto the terrace below. Motionless. From this position, he was medivaced out. Defeated. Meanwhile, the blackbird flew off in retreat.

Sadly, I cradled his crumpled body in my hand. I assumed he had broken his neck on impact and death was, therefore, instant.

As I stroked the soft warm feathers of his breast, I realised in all this time I had never before touched Dennis. A single feather detached itself from his broken body and burled along the flagstones of the terrace. I gently put him down, deciding to come back after breakfast and bury my former friend. As the little corpse was lowered back onto the wall, I blew him a goodbye kiss and turned to go…

When, as if by some miracle, Dennis's eye muscles began to quiver. Could this be true? Seconds later, one beady dark eye opened and Dennis was back from the dead! A wry smile across his face. As I watched, he began to resurrect himself, and in a matter of moments, he was performing the Dennis war dance on the top of the wall. Clearly, he wanted his victory roll to take place at the site of the battle.

Dennis, it transpired, had not lost his nerve or apparently his appetite. He fluttered along the wall to peck away at his morning meal, completely unruffled by events. A tiny modest hero consuming his 'Full Monty'.

Had he really managed to turn a failed attack into a coup? Had he, by any chance, feigned death to deceive the blackbird into retreat, and thereby retain his meal? Was it all part of a calculated military-style plan? Who is to tell…?

My own conclusion is: one should never underestimate a dunnock.

According to Luck

No more revision! My mother agreed a break would be 'just what the doctor ordered'. A healthy walk in the fresh air would be invigorating and help me prepare for my imminent clarinet examination.

As I sat on the gate, one of our cows came over. Gently, I stroked her broad nose, whereupon she threw back her head, catching my chin, driving two of my lower teeth through my upper lip. Two further teeth were jangling around in the blood that now filled my mouth.

Sorrowfully, I trudged homewards with a large handkerchief over my bleeding lip.

En route, I encountered a woman exercising a Labrador by harmlessly throwing a wooden stick to be retrieved. She swung round with full force, slipping in the mud, as she let go the stick. The branch hit me squarely on the cheekbone.

The blood gushed; luckily, my handkerchief was sufficient to cover both wounds.

Feeling rather dazed, I took the shortcut back.

Both hands being engaged in the mopping operation rendered me unable to save myself when I tripped crossing a ditch. I heard both wrists crack simultaneously.

The hospital afforded a diverse choice of possible venues: orthopaedic fracture clinic, dental emergencies or plain A & E. It was like having three party invitations—but all for the same evening!

Devastated, I sat on my hospital bed, glumly contemplating two unusable hands, a non-functioning mouth and awaiting stitches in my cheek.

In one agonising and incredibly unlucky afternoon, I had been robbed of all the faculties necessary to play my clarinet. It beggared belief.

It was at that moment my mother came over to me. She bent forward to comfort and encourage with the words:

"You could just take the theory exam, I suppose!"

In the Bleak Mid-Winter

Envisage if you will a National Hunt Race meeting somewhere in deepest darkest Southern England.

The grey January skies glowering overhead like a displeased dowager. The gloom is gathering as the afternoon racing continues in accordance with the race card.

The air is damp and still, yet aromatic whiffs of cigar smoke manage to steal across the small grandstand area dedicated to 'Owners and Trainers', and plummet down onto the bookmakers below.

The grass, the consistency of mushy peas and of a similar lifeless colour, squelches beneath your feet. The ground is confirmed as "heavy going".

A mature British winter's day in the countryside. The grey short days are so well practiced, they achieve virtually uniform results throughout the month. The level of light is beginning to fade, as two elderly people set out, ambling like badgers along the turf.

Meanwhile, striped horse blankets are being removed as jockeys and trainers enter the parade ring for last-minute instructions. The riders fidget nervously in front of their mounts and masters. A familiar smell of hot horse and an air of anticipation seems to pervade the tense expectant atmosphere.

The aforementioned octogenarian couple proceed steadily towards the Tote. Laden with members' badges, 'Time Form' books, race cards, 'The Sporting Life', field glasses and a shooting stick, they move stiffly towards their goal. He is tall and upright for his age, wearing a brown checked tweed suit and trilby hat.

The woman, of stout build and strong jawline, has a slight limp; no doubt a touch of arthritis is to blame. She also wears a brown hat of practical felt construction, the type favoured in the mid-1930s, designed to combat the most challenging winter weather. Surely this item would never become unseated! The durable nature of this millinery had much in common with her practical brogue footwear.

Steadfastly, they moved along and conversation is attempted. The reader should bear in mind that the two companions, although walking side-by-side, are roughly a third of an acre apart. Also, they are both sporting hearing aids – clearly, they are not operational.

Communications, not unlike the outdated use of flag signals at the battle of Jutland, have little hope of success. Quite understandable, given the field conditions on both of these occasions.

The duo continued trudging along; I overheard the following dialogue, intermittently delivered and at maximum volume:

Elderly lady: "I see Charles has Gawn."
Pregnant pause.
Elderly gent: "Gawn...dead, yer mean?"
Undaunted.
Elderly lady: "No, Gawn on holiday."

A lone blackbird breaks into his winter song trilling in amusement from a nearby hedge. This heroic attempt at conversation in which two people speak the same language and do not communicate, combined with their mutual lack of recognition of the inherent humour of the situation, puts this tale in the Winner's Enclosure time and time again.

However dire my situation, I have, for twenty years, always relied on this anecdote to bring a smile to my lips. Truly, I have enjoyed reliving this incident more than the 10/1 winner I had in the 3:15 later that day. Undoubtedly, its effects were both far more beneficial, and long-lasting!

Per Ardua ad Astra
Through Adversity to the Stars

Dedication

This tale is dedicated to all those who have ever helped the elderly.

Head bent low, she tackled the mounting pile of cards and envelopes on her writing desk. Methodically, she ticked off names from her list, as the pile of paperwork on her left began to escalate.

"Hello Nan! Just popped in to see what mischief you are up to!" I said with a smile.

Looking slowly upwards, she peered above the rim of her glasses, her eyes gradually focussing in recognition of her daughter.

"Just finishing writing my Christmas cards, darling," she said with enthusiasm. "Only 15 more to go!"

Peeping over her shoulder, I perused the list. Then gently pointed out that Aunty Winnie and Uncle Keith had died several years ago. It may be wise to remove them from the Christmas card list, I suggested cautiously. Unfazed, my mother responded in a flat tone: "I thought I hadn't heard from them recently."

She continued her hand-written festive greeting to the couple inside the card, in readiness to post. Finally, after a period of measured and serious consideration of the matter, she began to affix a second-class stamp, rather than her usual choice of first-class, on the card for the moribund pair. Speed of postal delivery being less critical in their particular circumstances.

She picked up the Christmas card list and scrutinised all the names; letting out a gentle sigh, she observed: "I don't know who any of these people are. Do you?"

She carried on with her task in silence. Meanwhile, I noticed she was wearing one purple velvet slipper with bow, and on the other foot, a mauve sports shoe. I contented myself with the fact that at least her footwear was on the same colour spectrum. *A fashion faux pas or just a matter of indecision?* I mused.

"Have I had lunch, dear?" she ventured.

I hesitated, wondering how to respond to this question, as I could not immediately think of any way I could possibly know the answer. It was not a problem I was regularly expected to face. Was there an unwritten law or clinical procedure by which daughters, by definition of their status, should instinctively know whether one's mother had lunched or not? If so, I had obviously missed this chapter. The answer had to be the sink. Sure enough, my detective work paid off as I witnessed an unwashed soup plate, spoon and saucepan lurking at the bottom of the Belfast sink.

"Yes," I said confidently, "you had soup."

Buoyed up with my recent success, after sniffing the debris, I confirmed: "Mushroom, I think."

It is worth noting that clairvoyance is a talent older people tend to expect from virtually all those they encounter. Never more so than with the current location of one's spectacles. More specifically, the TV glasses (green case), reading glasses (black case) and driving glasses (tan leather case). Keeping tabs on these essentials is worthy of an electronic tracking device for spectacles being developed, specifically for O.A.P.s. Or possibly some type of dynamic positioning via satellite could be employed to detect the whereabouts of these items. However, the current searching process on foot does have the benefit of burning up the calories, as you leap up and down the stairs in pursuit.

Despite a total knee replacement, asthma, swollen ankles, deafness (no hearing aid worn as it spoils one's hair) plus a host of other minor ailments, and not forgetting a recent cataract operation, my mother deemed herself fully sea-worthy, and thus fit to travel.

She glanced triumphantly in my direction and subsequently with feverish excitement began waving her certificate of travel insurance. Had she been awarded "Best in Show" at Chelsea Flower Show, the level of relish on her face could not have been greater. Determination ran deep in her veins; no mere insurance firm or travel company would be keen to banish her from International Departures. Take it from me, my intrepid and uncompromising mater would not easily be confined to the beaches of Bognor Regis.

After all, this was a woman who, as a teenager in 1943, had gone for a swim in the sea on the sunny southeast coast by crawling through the barbed-wire barrier fencing. This was for a dare, not even a bet! Later, she casually mentioned that the whole stretch of sand in question was heavily mined.

They bred them strong on Tyneside in 1930.

Although I can no longer claim to be a child, as I am facing my mid-sixties, travelling with my mother quite often reminds me of my childhood. Specifically, the complete recklessness of the older traveller. They appear blissfully unaware and quite oblivious of the mayhem they inadvertently cause. They manage to blaze along the trail regardless, and keep going…!

Those escorting an elderly family member overseas will appreciate exactly what is required when looking after those "ancients" who steadfastly will not drop anchor and continue to explore. The forbearance required is legion. The patience required is unfathomable. The resilience required is absolute.

Only those travelling companions who have chaperoned, and watched with amazement how their charges emerge from virtually every awkward situation unscathed, will fully comprehend this. I feel sure they will be enabled to both empathise and appreciate my anecdote. At this juncture, my introspection was interrupted by Nan's voice calling: "Where are my reading glasses, dear? I am planning a holiday in the Greek islands, and I need them now…" Her voice trailed away…

6 months later

It was in the wee small hours before Special Assistance passenger's check-in opened that Nan decided she needed the loo. In the nick of time, I managed to retrieve her by the coat collar as her hand hit the handle of the gents' lavatory door. As if on auto-pilot, she rescheduled her visit. Head down and determination etched on her face, she redirected herself towards the ladies.

It proved hard to find a maintenance mechanic at 2:40 am willing to enter the ladies' toilet. Flourishing his toolbox like Pandora, he attempted to rescue Nan from her self-imposed imprisonment within the cubicle. He assured me, with a good headwind, she could be in with a sporting chance of catching the flight. This was despite the fact the lock was so severely jammed he would need to uplift the entire door. Although, thankfully, not the frame as well!

His prognosis proved sound.

Shortly after this interlude, she was whisked via buggy and subsequently wheelchair onto the platform lift on the outside of the plane. The platform had restraining belts fitted to secure the "chariots" to the side panels for safety. Rather like horses tethered in stalls within a stable.

The lift began, jerkily, to move upwards before the chariots had been fastened. The effect was noteworthy. All six chariots, plus their animated occupants, began slithering to and fro across the platform. Airily, they waved their walking sticks above their heads, akin to triumphant warriors with battle axes being wheeled aloft after a long and arduous siege. They lurched, zoomed and hurtled in all directions. All the while cheering like 10-year-olds in bumper cars. These unsecured vehicles were the source of more spontaneous fun than any carefully planned itinerary at an exotic holiday location.

I am confident most of the charioteers had more enjoyment from this incident than from their entire forthcoming holiday!

At this point I reminded myself, with some trepidation, that all these antics had occurred both in quick succession and even before take-off!

Once on-board the aircraft, the indefatigable Nan, having watched the stewardess perform the safety briefing, reached for her life jacket under the seat and in a flash it was inflated! Not content with pulling the toggle on the garment, she began to experiment with the whistle! As for me, sadly, there was absolutely nowhere to hide.

Later the same day

Recovering in the afternoon sunshine beside the hotel pool, I was concerned when Nan was tempted to "take to the waters", and thereafter, naturally, wanted to remove her wet swimsuit. She requested I hold a towel in front of her to save walking to the changing area; I duly obliged.

In our corner of the garden, we were not overlooked and the floor-to-ceiling hotel window behind her had the curtains firmly drawn across. To ensure complete privacy, I noted there was not a chink in the window covering. Soaking wet, she shimmered in the sunlight and with me dutifully holding the towel to her front as protection, she pulled down her costume. Just as the swimwear fell to her ankles, the unthinkable happened. In an instant, the curtain behind her drew back electrically. There, seated in the vast room, were 250 conference delegates from the Chinese National Oil Corporation, all facing directly towards her, naked and not insubstantial rear end. My inevitable comment: "Nan, don't turn around just now," had the predictable result. Of course, she turned 180 degrees. In consequence, 250 stunned Orientals now had a clear idea of every aspect of her uncovered body.

My few woefully inadequate words of consolation floated away unheard…mea culpa.

Nevertheless, her steely resolve to enjoy our holiday carried on unabated. Later that evening at our suave hotel, there was to be held a cocktail reception.

We were chatting to the establishment's management team; Nan was talking to the General Manager at the time. The smile on the man's face seemed permanently fixed throughout the party. Until I saw his face fall for the first time that evening. In a trice he found himself facing an "urgent situation" that required his immediate and personal intervention. Thus he escaped! Had news reached him of the swimsuit escapade? Could this have provoked an international incident? I speculated.

So swiftly did he take his leave and "abandon ship" that I came over to ask Nan what seemed to be the problem. What emergency was about to befall us? What had caused him to shoot off so unexpectedly?

Was there a fire?

Were terrorists afoot and about to attack?

Was the Chinese delegation about to take reprisals, I wondered out loud.

"No, I don't think so, dear, I was just telling the fellow how much we are enjoying our stay," she chortled. "I said I would love to return and plan to book the second visit for this autumn. Strange how he dashed off without explanation. Most odd," she surmised.

It was clear to me at least, her reputation went before her, and I was reminded of T.S. Eliot's *Growltiger's Last Stand*,

The cottagers of Rotherhithe knew something of his fame;
At Hammersmith and Putney people shuddered at his name.
They would fortify the hen-house, lock up the silly goose,
When the rumour ran along the shore: GROWLTIGER'S
ON THE LOOSE!

Any accompanying daughter would shudder at the prospect of their octogenarian charge heading for the travel section of "The Telegraph", let alone the check-in desk. Saga staff have reportedly resigned at the mention of her name. The term "travel sickness", I believe, refers not to the traveller's physical symptoms, it is a strain of worry-induced spasms only experienced by those accompanying the stubborn older traveller that causes the symptoms. Namely, nervous anxiety and a constant fear of impending disaster.

I feel sure these words will strike a chord with daughters and chaperones everywhere! To conclude my travelogue, it goes without saying that my inveterate mother continued to sail unscathed like a Spanish galleon through our adventure abroad. There is a lesson here to be learned by the younger generation.

Perhaps mastering old age and becoming a 'successful ancient' is epitomised by handling the challenges of travel.

The key factors are unquestionably an unyielding approach to all obstacles combined with a stubborn refusal to give in, plus a firm belief in the value of enjoying oneself.

Be irrepressible is the message.

Speaking for myself, my own learning outcome is far more prosaic: I have developed a very deep, even profound, appreciation of a stiff margarita.

Part 2

The Challenge

"Five and twenty ponies
Trotting through the dark –
Brandy for the Parson,
'Baccy for the Clerk.
Laces for a lady; letters for a spy,
Watch the wall my darling, while the Gentlemen go by!"

'A Smuggler's Song', Rudyard Kipling, 1906.

The Romney Marshes Kent, 1938.
The marsh is a mysterious place. First rising to notoriety as the haunt of smugglers in the 18th century, who worked from the town of Rye and the original Cinque Ports on the Kent Sussex coastline.

It is also home to the famed Romney sheep, which graze its fertile grassland.

A low-lying area, it is frequently shrouded in sea mist and fog. It has an eerie magical feel; an atmosphere all of its own. However, it is not to everyone's taste.

It was spine chilling to think this was just the place where any invasion force from Europe would land.

Standing and leaning up against the bar, my father was enjoying a well-earned drink. It had been a successful day's shooting over his new spaniel, who had worked like a Trojan. Charlie had earned his spurs today. With more than a few difficult water retrieves under his belt, he was confident the dog was going to be a winner. A warm glow flushed his cheeks; he felt a peaceful contentment in the quiet of the rural bar room. There he was able to relax and reflect on the day's sport undisturbed.

The landlord had other ideas. He didn't like to see an interesting new face enjoying his own company. In his role as a mine host, he felt bound to intrude by way of convivial conversation.

Reluctantly, father was drawn into discussion. Inevitably, the political situation in Europe would be on the agenda.

A local dealer-farmer was the only other patron at the bar. In addition, a shrivelled older man sat alone, at a circular table, tapping his bar mat. This was his customary seat, perfectly positioned to overhear any tittle-tattle or gossip from the customers at the bar.

At this time, much seasonal work in the locality was carried out by itinerant workers. It seemed that the whole of the east end of London emptied into Kent for the hop-picking season in September. Strawberries were harvested in late spring, followed by other varieties of soft fruit, through to apple picking in early autumn. Children joined in during the summer holidays, and travelling gypsy folk became part of the temporary and roving workforce. The work was highly weather dependent. Even as a child in the mid-fifties and early sixties, I remember, these armies of urban pickers were viewed as a 'mixed blessing'.

It was not uncommon for items of value to go missing on a permanent basis after their farm work. Hens, eggs, tools of any value would be a forfeit the landowner had to pay to recruit the quantity of short-term labour needed. One could not afford to be choosy, as often fruit pickers were needed at point blank notice; before the perishables perished! For the farmer, this situation represented a double-edged sword.

Gypsies were seen as a last resort in a labour crisis, as they were termed 'light-fingered' and generally less reliable. Poaching was rife amongst them, and they earned a reputation for playing havoc with the countryside as their camps were squalid with litter and debris, which was scattered far and wide.

The gypsy women sold their wares, wooden pegs, crochet work, bunches of wild flowers on a door-to-door basis in the villages. Generally speaking, they proved unpopular and were classed as vagabonds. Frequently, they were sent packing empty handed.

The dealer drinking at the end of the bar was an uncouth man. A burly, sweaty, corpulent figure, his belly spilled out over the top of his belt. His thick neck gave him the distinct look of a bully and he possessed the temperament to match.

He exhibited all the hallmarks of a troublemaker.

Beneath the low roof of the hostelry, the door creaked open uneasily. Stooping under the lintel, a lanky individual entered. His black wavy hair was greasy, and he wore a dirty cloth jacket and waistcoat. Leather gaiters covered most of his ragged trousers and a clay pipe poked out of his breast pocket. He possessed a brown lined face stained with dirt, and was of indeterminate age, neither young nor old. Both his demeanour and his clothes exhibited a well-worn look.

He took up a chair by the fireside. Stretching his long legs straight out in front of him, the heels of his hobnail boots rested on the brick floor of the bar room.

Meanwhile, my father was explaining to the publican how the fact he had a Private Pilot's Licence, had helped in his acceptance to the RAF next month as a potential pilot officer. He was aiming to be a fighter pilot before too long, and joining up for peacetime service – at least to start with – he was now looking forward to his new career.

The dealer eyed the dark stranger suspiciously.

As a local landowner, he was not fond of gypsies. Effectively addressing the old man at the table, he began, indirectly, provoking the new arrival. On the attack he landed his first blow by stating that casual labour should be renamed 'lay about labour'. He followed on by maintaining the gypsies were 'thieving magpies' incapable of doing a decent day's work for their pay.

The gypsy made no response to these and other taunts.

Finally, he goaded the sitter by the fireplace by adding that if war was declared tomorrow, you wouldn't see a single gypsy on the front line. Concluding, "You wouldn't see their tails' for dust!" Antagonistically, he then began to sing:

"Run Rabbit, Run"

Clearly, he was angling to have the man thrown out, or ensure he left of his own accord. The landlord stepped in at this point. In proprietorial manner, he attempted to diffuse the situation. A short but awkward pause ensued. Deflected, but undeterred the dealer changed tactics.

Loud mouthed as ever, he claimed to own the fiercest crossbred dog in the country. Apparently, he had recently bought it to guard against pilfering by gypsies and other undesirables. In his usual rumbustious style, he gave assurances that the dog would attack anyone entering his property. It was invincible!

"I defy anyone to get past that dog from my gate to the front door!" he claimed. "I would willingly give a £5 note to anyone who could!" he finished with gusto.

Not once had the gypsy spoken until this point. Without looking up, he said in a soft Irish accent: "I will."

The challenge was set.

My father was drafted in as adjudicator. By all accounts, if the man was brought down by this huge brute of a dog, it was bound to tear out his throat. A gruesome fact that the dealer seemed to revel in, adding with alacrity, the dog had neither food nor drink that day. My father brought with him his gun, as a precautionary measure. He hoped he would not have to use it.

In the yard, behind the house, was a large wooden barrel. It was lying on its side, half-filled with straw; it formed the dog's kennel. From the dog's wide collar, a strong metal chain was attached, which served to anchor the beast. The empty food and water bowls were just out of reach of the chain at its fullest extent.

The gladiator was salivating, and wrenching violently against the chain. Enough to deter all, but the most persistent caller!

By now, the sun was sinking towards the skyline, and hobnail boots could be heard clipping along the lane. Just as darkness fell, the gypsy met my father at the gate. It was pointed out to him what was required. He had to climb the gate, and cross the ground leading to the pathway, to reach the porch. The front door would be left ajar, so a guiding indoor light could be seen. If he met the challenge, he would gain his reward. The combatant nodded his understanding without hesitation.

Duly, the dog was let loose.

Sitting astride the gate, the gypsy slipped noiselessly to the ground.

Straining relentlessly at the chain seemed to have exhausted the creature temporarily. Released, and able to move freely, he stood stock-still! Sauntering towards the empty feed bowls, he licked them wistfully. Then he took a few steps and cocked his ears, he was listening intently. Moving his head to the right and left, he tentatively sniffed the air. All the while, he was slobbering. He was both hungry and angry. A savage opponent to behold.

Given the darkness, it was hard to tell what progress, if any, the gypsy had made. Or indeed where he was.

The dog took one more deep sniff, pawed the ground and moved slowly towards the entrance gate. Never once did he bark. The chain, which was still attached to the dog's collar, made an ominous dragging sound, and also gave a clear indication of the dog's whereabouts.

Several minutes elapsed. No tortured sounds from either party were audible – just the sound of the chain dragging across the yard. All of a sudden, the dog burst into action pounding towards the gate and letting out a deep throated baying, as he rushed to protect his territory. It must have been a blood curdling noise to anyone close by. Especially, if you were unarmed, and not even wearing protective clothing!

Equally unnerving was the ensuing silence.

What on earth could be happening?

In the clear night air, the panting of the dog could be heard as he steadfastly stalked his prey.

By now, father was beginning to curse the stupid challenge and was genuinely wishing he had not become involved.

The odds were so heavily stacked against the gypsy.

Somewhere in the darkness, came the slight sound of muffled movement from 'the human sacrifice' and this was backed up by a low moaning. The gypsy was moving forward. The dog was standing still.

Had the tables turned?

My father witnessed the dog's reaction on nearing the gypsy. It was beyond belief.

The animal dropped its vast bulk to the ground, its hair bristling, its body cowering and shivering simultaneously. All the while, it made a plaintive whimpering cry. It lay completely still. Beaten. There was not a mark on its body! Rising, tail between its legs, it began to slink away defeated. It was a miraculous sight. Spellbinding. My father was speechless.

By now, the gypsy had reached the porch. Standing to his full height, he appeared to be dusting down his trousers and jacket. A hand extended from the half open door, it held a large white £5 note. The dealer hadn't got the courage to come out and congratulate the gypsy on his victory.

The two men in the garden met in the darkness. Smiling, they warmly shook hands. A bond of mutual respect now bound them.

My father suggested a celebratory drink at the pub. The gypsy replied: "No, sir, I'll not be accepting drinks from strangers."

My father was rather taken aback by his response.

"You must tell me…" he began, "how…?"

"There is nothing to it sir. To be sure, nothing at all," the gypsy assured him.

Baffled, my father let it go. Together, they walked along the lane. The gypsy began chewing tobacco; he was in no hurry to go anywhere.

"It's like this, sir," he eventually mustered, "a dog must see a man's eye before he attacks. Contact with the eye is the thing," he continued. "I made sure he couldn't see mine."

Still my father was perplexed. The gypsy spat out his chewing tobacco carelessly.

"On all fours, with my jacket over my head and neck, I crawled to the door. All the while, I made a wailing sound." My father considered this incredible information before his rejoinder, "However you did it, a great deal of courage was required."

"No, sir," said the gypsy, "it's you that have the courage, to fight in aeroplanes."

Nobody said anything further.

A short while later, the gypsy turned from the lane towards the field housing their Romany caravans. Before he branched off, addressing my father again in his lyrical Irish accent, he said:

"May your God preserve you, sir."

Luckily, for my father, he did just that. Thankfully, he must have been a listening God!

Out of the Blue

"Can you come to London with me tomorrow?" said the voice at the end of the telephone line. "To do some shopping," he added as an afterthought.

"Why? Can't you choose your own knickers and socks," I replied jokingly.

"No, it's not that sort of shopping. I need a female's input."

"I thought you were going to ask me to Brands Hatch or something exciting," I said. "London in the summer is just for tourists. Besides, I am going up to University next week, and I have got masses to do."

It had been a glorious summer, and I was on a roll. A holiday job for just one month to earn some cash, staying with friends in Devon, swimming in the sea and after long walks, drinking cider in village pubs with thatched rooves. All this was blessed with unbelievable weather.

Best of all, the A' Level results. I was still euphoric, as I was now able to take up a place at my first choice University. To cap all this, there had been several eighteenth birthday parties over the holidays, including one triple eighteenth, which stood out from the crowd. Golden days indeed!

I was now ready to leave home, and had the 'bit between my teeth' to start a new era in my life. I needed an invigorating challenge; fresher's week was only a few days away now, and I couldn't wait to start life as a student.

Peter continued, "Did you know Pa has won the Queen's Award for Industry?"

"No, when was it announced?" I asked with sincere interest. Ignoring the question, Peter moved on saying,

"Pa has asked me to buy something special for mother to mark the occasion. Will you help?"

"Yes, of course," I replied. "Where shall we meet?"

"I'll be heading for Bond Street," said Peter. "I'll see you outside the Ritz."

"Why don't we make it Fortnum's, then you can buy me a coffee and explain what you have in mind?"

"It's a deal. See you there at 11am," he concluded the phone call and replaced the receiver.

Peter Fortesque-Brown was diametrically opposite in every respect to both his parents. He was naturally shy, introspective and rather dull. A 21-year-old man, who was overshadowed by his successful father, and paled into insignificance in front of his formidable mother. He was the type who went unnoticed in a crowd. He was always the outsider in any group. To date, he has meandered apathetically through his life and had very little to show for his twenty-one years on the planet.

Through choice, he would probably not have been a friend; we had precious little in common. My family were not wealthy like Peter's, but unlike Peter, I made a point of enjoying every opportunity that came my way. I thrived at school, where I never had time to take up all the sports and hobbies on offer. One of the reasons I spent time with Peter and his family was that Peter's father was my father's key client. Our parents were close friends, and given that they lived nearby, I had constant contact with the Fortesque-Brown's for all my eighteen years.

His father, who spent every day, and most evenings at their increasingly successful light engineering firm, had despaired of Peter displaying any interest in the company. Joining the family business was not on Peter's agenda. Secretly, his father was relieved. After all what could Peter do?

Peter's mother, Greta, had been a tall proud figure of a woman. A hunting accident had left her wheelchair dependant. Thus, she spent all her time in their extensive family home. On fine days, you would inevitably see her enveloped in a Hermes headscarf on the terrace, from where she could savour the delights of the gardens. Etched in my subconscious was an image of her depicted as 'Queen Mary in a go-kart'. She had austerity imprinted on her personality. Her severe features, strength of purpose and air of authority gave her personal resources of the strongest mettle. Her face showed the power of endurance (born of frequent pain I wondered). I sensed that she recognised some of these qualities in me, albeit to a lesser extent. I always thought Greta was considering me mouldable in terms of potential daughter-in-law material. In short, there was common ground between us. To some extent, we were kindred spirits.

It would be fair to say that Peter's upbringing had been fairly hands off throughout his twenty odd years. His father's long working days, I suspect, were initially to escape his wife, and he had happily let the job take over his life. Greta had little time for Peter, regarding him as 'no use to man or beast'. Alternatively, 'neither use nor ornament'. She made it obvious that Peter was a great disappointment in her life. They were very ill-assorted.

Peter's near emotional starvation at home, added to his ill-advised schooling, compounded to blight his character, and make worse his social awkwardness.

It was his mother, who instigated Peter's name being put forward to the boarding school, where Churchill was educated, in the firm belief this would toughen him up. Actually, five years of this education caused Peter to retreat further into his shell. It only served to confirm his suspicions that he was no good at academic work, hopeless at sport, had no talent for art and in general, disliked being part of a highly competitive all-male society. In fact, Peter hated his schooling to such an extent, he had swallowed a two-inch iron nail just prior to being driven back to commence the new term. By this means, he managed to miss two days of school. He always maintained the risk was most definitely worth the reward!

Greta's theory was, perhaps after a spell of working abroad, to wherever the family could banish him, Peter might return enlightened. Which would obviously mean, he would keenly enter the family business on his return to the fold. One could only pray the boy would come to his senses… Despite his mother's numerous overseas connections, her notion of sending the boy abroad to widen his horizons and make a man of him, came to an abrupt halt when she realised the East India Company was no longer actively recruiting. Or indeed trading.

Why had no one told her?

Ultimately, given the young man's genuine lack of interest in almost everything (with the slight exception of motor racing), a decision was reached on Peter's behalf. Presumably, on the basis of Peter occasionally taking their dog, Pilot, for a walk in the grounds and farmland near the Fortesque-Brown residence, it was assumed that he might enjoy both walking and the countryside. Peter's father duly instructed his secretary to book Peter into the Royal College of Agriculture in Cirencester. Thus, his future was determined. When told of his father's decision regarding his career, Peter merely nodded, outwardly indifferent to the idea. As far as Peter was concerned, the college was favourably close to Silverstone, which was the only plus factor.

Unlike his parents, instead of diminishing him, I had the opposite effect on Peter. He seemed comfortable in my presence. We were both only children, yet he seemed to view me as a little sister! Certainly, he appeared more confident and outgoing with me for company, and much happier away from his parents and home.

Meeting as agreed, we wandered slowly down Bond Street after having visited the bank in Piccadilly to finalise the bankers' draft arrangements. We entered a shop midway down the street. They appeared to be expecting us; I imagined an appointment had been made prior to our visit. We were shown into the ring room, where lights beamed from every direction.

An impeccably dressed representative of the company, after explaining a few security measures, appeared with trays of rings for our inspection. The sales person made the understandable mistake of assuming Peter was buying the ring for me. Unfortunately, Peter said,

"Oh! No, no, no, it's not for this lady. It is for another lady. About the same size and colouring. She's just here to try it on, for fit!"

The strange mixture of embarrassment and empathy which crossed the salesman's face was quite astonishing.

It did not take too long to find what we were looking for. A magnificent sapphire, a fabulous stone, which stood out from the rest. It was the deepest blue, set in diamonds with a platinum shank.

"It's the most beautiful stone Peter," I said with conviction. I tried it on and looked at it in the various mirrors available. The assistant told Peter a few details regarding the piece and by this stage, I didn't want to take it off!

"Greta will love it. She's bound to," I said. So it was agreed to purchase the ring as a gift from husband to wife and thereby celebrate a career pinnacle. Reluctantly, I removed the ring, and handed it over. Peter watched me closely, and suddenly came up with an idea.

"Why don't I buy you a replica if you like it so much? It will be a fake I'm afraid though. Call it a gift for achieving your University place," he added.

"Only, don't wear it in front of mother!" was his parting shot.

The replication service took twenty-four hours, so the next day, Peter collected the ring.

Both items were encased in small red leather boxes, and then placed into a plain carrier bag.

That evening, a formal reception for a few senior staff from the business and close family members was held at Cheviot Hall. Greta, I understand was overwhelmed with her husband's present, which was also a perfect fit.

Peter had driven to my house in his Porsche in order to escape the ordeal of the party. When he arrived, he handed me a small red leather box.

"It's not worth much," he said candidly. "But it might stop someone, wearing a bear skin and cudgel, from dragging you off to their cave, when you take it north next week!"

"I'm not going to University husband-hunting," I retorted. "You know me better than that surely? I want a career."

"Ah! Yes, a career. I have heard that somewhere before – you sound just like my father!" We both laughed together.

"What did you give your folks?" I enquired.

"I gave Pa a special bottle of Krug," he replied.

"Your mother, what did you give her?" I added.

His baby features, full cheeks, and exceptionally curly blond hair took on a look I had never seen on his face before. His eyes narrowed, and it was an expression of pure malice.

"A book," he replied coldly. "You know she has never been a mother to me."

I experienced a frisson.

Then a deep feeling of disquiet surged over my body.

My mother spotted the ring within fifteen seconds of me entering the room.

The inevitable, "Where did that come from? You can't wear that. It's an engagement ring", and other predictable comments, culminating in "You will have to give it back!" Resulted in me storming out of the room. The same concerns were echoed by my father later; he viewed the main problem being the prospect of losing his best client, and best friend in one. I held my own, explaining it was a replica, and I was not giving it back. It was a relatively valueless gift from an old friend. It was mine. Enough said.

The weekend before fresher's week, we were due to stay with my uncle and aunt for a few days. Uncle Joe held a patriarchal role in the family, by virtue of the fact he was the oldest surviving member. He had reached that enviable point in his career where he could pick and choose among his private patients, and so only worked as he wished. Subsequently, he and his wife were able to visit their daughter in South Africa for three months every year. Lately, he had mellowed down and become more tolerant, or so I had thought until he began to intervene in the issue of the ring.

The other house guests were due to arrive shortly; a couple my relatives had met in Johannesburg, Leslie and Anne. They were briefly visiting my aunt and uncle, and the rest of the week, Leslie would be working in London. He was a diamond merchant.

Everyone seemed to agree my ring was lovely and very realistic. They could not believe I had been given it 'out of the blue'. No strings attached.

"I've seen and worn the original," I said. "That's a real bobby-dazzler!"

The diamond merchant could see my distress when the issue of returning the ring was raised again.

When I burst out, "I don't care if it's real or not, I just love the colour and the eye catching design. It is mine!"
I felt Leslie was misreading the situation; it became clear to me he was thinking I was secretly engaged. He tried to allay the family quarrel and help me at the same time. Having said there were a great deal of hard to detect replicas on the market, and that sapphires were not his speciality, he agreed to take the gemstone ring to London on Monday for an analysis and valuation. This had stopped what had developed into a family feud in its tracks.

By the time Monday evening came, the situation had been diffused, and nobody seemed too worried about the outcome of the analysis. After dinner, Leslie said, over coffee, that it was a good replica – but definitely a replica – and as such, it had a limited value, as costume jewellery. That was the end of the matter.

Just before I went to bed, Leslie followed me out of the room and handed me an envelope.

"I thought you might like to keep the report and official verdict," he said. "It is a description of the item and the tests carried out. Keep it, just for the record," he concluded.

I thanked him as I disappeared down the corridor.

In the privacy of my bedroom, I thought I would have a quick look at the document and opened the envelope. There were several pages covering the technical details, so I turned to the final page, which was a valuation for insurance purposes. My tired eyes scanned the text…rare stone…exceptional quality…replacement value £22,500.

My initial reaction was disbelief. Followed by shock and dismay in that order. Peter must have swapped the stones. Was he paying Greta back deliberately? Was it a genuine mistake? I was now facing a major dilemma. He had left me in a quandary. I decided to do nothing until I had spoken with Peter.

The following morning, I packed and left on an early train to start my new life in the north.

Earlier, we had agreed that after I had settled in, Peter would come and visit, sometime during my first term.

"It will give the Porsche a good run, a round trip of six-hundred miles," he had said. "I suppose I might stand you a beer and a sandwich too!"

He had sent me a note asking to visit the following weekend as he had something he particularly wanted to ask me. What was he proposing?

I never found out.

He was killed outright on the A1 northbound. A head-on collision.

Was it to admit he had made a mistake, and wanted me to return the ring?

Was it to confess he had made the swap on purpose, and thereby revenge his mother?

Could it be a more personal issue?

It seemed to me the answers to all these questions no longer mattered.

However, my tale does explain one thing.

How I ended up with an engagement ring and no fiancée.

Tipping Point: A Story in Four Parts

'If I ever marry anyone, it will be him', was my spontaneous reaction.

I looked straight at him as I passed by. He did not look up. I went unnoticed.

This was the first time I saw him, striding across the wide entrance hallway of the Student Union – great coat flapping open, unfastened.

I. September

Returning early for the autumn term was the norm for serious rowers. The first VIII usually spent the entire summer up at University to concentrate on their sport.

I had made sure my fitness and stamina was maintained over the long summer vacation with regular trips to the gym and runs. The majority of competitive oarsmen were medical students, so by and large they were already based at University and at the local hospitals, and could continue their outings as a crew.

Celia, the stroke of our ladies IV walked down to the water, which was tidal, to review the water conditions.

"Come and look at this," she said.

I followed down the steps to the water's edge. It was not an uncommon sight, more of a regular nuisance factor, to see all the various sized lumps of wood floating in the river. This always happened after a ship had been launched from dry dock. The tide sent the flotsam upstream, which can be very damaging to delicate boats.

The familiar dank smell of the river water greeted my nostrils, as crossing the wet floor of the boathouse I looked up at the racks upon racks of boats. Eights, fours, double skulls, single skulls and more besides. I noticed a new single skull boat – an expensive carbon fibre creation on one of the racks.

"That's new," I said. "Where did that come from?"

"It doesn't belong to the Boat Club," she replied. "It is privately owned."

The boat was called 'Walter Mitty'.

We walked back together to get kitted-up for our outing. Nearly all the club members arrived by a forty-two seater coach, which was provided to transport students the three plus miles from University to the Club.

It was very unusual for anyone not to come and go by this link. Personally, I always enjoyed the coach journey, which somehow added to the excitement and aura of rowing with my crew for the University. The travel was all part of the build-up for action.

I heard a scrunching of tyres on gravel outside the sliding doors of the main boathouse, and looked up to witness a Volkswagen Beetle parked there. The owner was heading purposefully towards the rack containing the 'Walter Mitty'.

Oddly, he was wearing shorts and wellington boots, topped by a great coat that was flapping, unfastened. He was also whistling an unfamiliar tune.

After our practice, my body was sweating although my hands were frozen and sore with blisters. My feet had been wet for most of the afternoon. The downside of rowing! Like so many tough physical activities, the troubles only begin when you stop! I had bright pink cheeks and knees to match, but at least my level of fitness wasn't a problem.

For the first outing of the season, we had done well. I felt a satisfying glow of achievement warming me inside.

I began daydreaming of the hot tea and jam sandwiches (it was always the same unidentifiable red jam) that Jimmy the Boatman was no doubt preparing for our arrival at the club bar.

There was also something else dwelling on my mind.

A *tête-a-tête* was required. Time to tackle Celia!

"Who is the new member? The one that owns the 'Walter Mitty'," I started, trying to sound casual.

"He's not new. You won't have met him. He had a year out last year to train with the World Champion in New Zealand. He's back on the course now, for his final year," she answered. "He's the best oarsman we'll ever have. He rowed for Eton, and won the Diamond Skulls at Henley. He's also a prospect for the Olympics. An absolute fanatic; he trains five nights a week, and does circuits every lunch time."

I was about to continue my investigation when she interrupted my train of thought.

"Why all the interest?" her perplexed expression didn't last long, as it gave way to a half smile.

"Ah!" she said knowingly.

Celia was also captain of the women's Boat Club, and being in her third year of medicine was now termed 'clinical'. As such, she was partly hospital-based.

I changed the subject rather obviously, by asking how life in nightshift A & E was treating her. She replied,

"Half the injuries are self-inflicted, which is a real frustration."

She wasn't shocked by this revelation, merely sounding disappointed. As a second year and still a teenager, who didn't hail from the elevated ranks of the medical school, all I could provide was a sympathetic ear.

"Everyone will be going to Martin's twenty-first, at The Bay Horse, next weekend. That will give you a chance to meet your man. I'll introduce you if you like," she volunteered. Clearly, she had given our previous topic of conversation some thought.

"But I warn you rowing is the only thing in his life. He's a fanatic. I don't fancy your chances. He's also pretty keen on combines and balers," she added as a final quip.

"Really," I said with gravity.

"He's just not the type that's interested in females. He knows they exist, but doesn't recognise there's a difference!"

"Obviously not a medic then!" I replied dryly. We both laughed.

"No, he's an agricultural engineer."

Her advice on one level was good. However, she was quite wrong about one thing, as I found to my chagrin. He did not show up to Martin's birthday party.

II. October

Bedecked in a backless, boned and borrowed full-length ball gown, belonging to a friend of a friend, I was off to the Medics Ball. It was a grand annual affair held at the Civic Centre and I was thrilled to have been asked. The dress had been severely modified by me at the last minute, with the aid of a staple gun, as I had realised far too late that it did not fit in any direction. Added to which, it was too long, so I would have been unable to dance, in fact, I would be in severe danger of breaking my neck should I be required to move at all!

This I vowed would not be the case at the Boat Club Dinner, for which I resolved to buy the dress of my dreams.

The Ball was a glittering occasion. I was beginning to enjoy my elevated social standing by moving in circles that were so august. Even though most of my friends were medics, they were a notoriously cliquish bunch. It was hard for anyone on the outside to break into their clannish fraternity. It seemed that I was now adopted into 'the firm'.

The son of the professor of rheumatology was a twenty-four year old undergraduate from Cambridge, who had rowed for ISIS, and transferred north for a year. He was about to become our new captain of men's rowing, as he was a much respected and commanding young man. Clever, well-connected and a physical giant; he was not someone who 'slipped under the radar'. He was engaged to another medical student called Janet Strachan, who incidentally did not row.

Marching up to our table, much to my surprise, and to the complete consternation of those at my table, he asked me to dance. Naturally, I was flattered and impressed by his direct approach. I was under the distinct impression by his manner that he was not often turned down!

Distracted by his attention and his self-assurance, I said, "Yes."

His practised charm was charismatic, and it seemed as we took to the dance floor that all eyes were upon us.

Feeling more than a little out of my depth, I said unwisely, "I thought you were engaged to Janet…"

"I was," he admitted blandly. "Let's dance."

How to deal with this straightforward and very public display of changed affection, I wondered. My sights were set firmly, true enough, but elsewhere!

The level of angst directed at me from Janet, who was still seated at their table, was frightening. I could feel her eyes boring through my backless dress. I just hoped after she qualified she did not become my local G.P. God forbid!

"Why did you call off your engagement?" I asked imprudently.

Without hesitation, he responded, "Because it is you that I want." I literally could not believe my ears. I hardly knew the guy.

After a couple more dances, I returned to my table, dazed. I did not invite him to join us, as I had a gut feeling that Janet might be sharpening her scalpel and coming our way. His overt strategy and forthright actions were an unprecedented experience in my case. I was completely at a loss!

The others at the table were agog with interest. How did I know Rob Walker? Me, being a non-medic, it seemed to them fantastic, like a fairy tale. I was also able to detect a little envy, mixed with a lot of jealousy, at least from the females present.

I was trying to explain he was just someone I knew through rowing, and at the same time give the impression that this type of occurrence happened to me quite regularly.

Nobody believed a word I said.

My own amorous ambitions remained, but only on the drawing board.

My lean, fair-haired, and wiry oarsman remained elusive. As he didn't travel to our twice weekly training sessions on the water by coach, I did not encounter him en route. Whenever we were at the Clubhouse after rowing, there were always flocks of keen Freshers eager for his advice on technique and fitness training, circling round him like over-enthusiastic sheep dogs.

So much time, or so it felt, had gone by since he had first caught my eye, and I had never once spoken to him, as yet! I ensured virtually every route I took on foot in my daily perambulations round the campus, included passing the Agriculture Building. So much time did I expend in this activity that Professor Weeks actually asked me if I was hoping to be accepted into the faculty!

Alas! My idol did not seem to either enter or leave the building, at least by any conventional methods. Perhaps he was airlifted in? It was baffling to say the least! To top it all, he never seemed to be at any Boat Club members' parties.

Did he know he was worshipped from afar?

I had a mission, which was also becoming something of a challenge. In retrospect, this was an understatement. In biblical terms, parting the Red Sea would have been an easier option.

My instinct told me that the formal dinner held annually and organised only for Club members was THE event no one missed. He just had to be there. Now everything rested on the Boat Club dinner. That was not until mid-December!

Jimmy, who looked after the Boat Club premises had worked in the nearby armaments factory for an entire lifetime. He was slender and pale-faced and coughed with regular monotony. The poor housing and constant damp of river fog from October through to March had played havoc with his breathing. He had a lovely open face; he could not be anything else but honest. Since his retirement, he had kept a careful eye on the Club and the contents of the Boathouse. It was a tough area, and the job entailed a good deal of night work.

He keenly handled any boat repair work, and despite his health problems was the ideal maintenance/caretaker.

He invariably wore a flat cap with a white scarf knotted at his throat. He thereby looked perfectly dressed to take part in another Jarrow March at a moment's notice. Of course, it was quite possible, chronologically, that he took part in the first one!

One measure of his popularity with members, if this was ever in any doubt, was the relative ease in obtaining contributions to Jimmy's Christmas box.

One of the greatest joys for me at the boathouse nestled next to the ladies' locker room. It was a magnificent 1920's enamel bath supported on four short stubby legs. It took an age to fill, but what a treat! So much more preferable to the rows of showers. This lovely old piece also enjoyed the privacy of closed doors behind it; it was quite unlike the open run of showers in every way.

It was Wednesday afternoon, which is reserved for sport and recreation at University. Our crew were unusually the first in from the water, walking the boat up the steps on the riverbank and tossing the boat, keel towards the river, we were rewarded by Jimmy having placed the trestles out, on which we rested the boat while hosing it down.

A severe bout of chesty coughing heralded the proximity of Jimmy onto the scene, who began calling in his customary hoarse tones: "Come on ladies, please, make way for the first VIII coming in. Hurry up now."

I was only too ready to oblige. A soak in that fabulous bath was uppermost in my mind: "Doctor's orders!"

I rushed up the stairs, ripping off my top as I went, hurriedly entering the ladies' changing area. I pulled off my remaining clothes. No time for lockers.

What I needed was a hot bath – and quickly, before too many others had the same idea.

Now, in my birthday suit, I speedily tiptoed over the cold red ochre tiles to the bathroom. I opened the door. It was apparent that it was already occupied, and slightly steamy. Filling the entire bath was the new Captain of the men's Boat Club, lying full-length and naked.

As I stopped point blank at the side of the bath, he slowly rose up to his statuesque height of 6 foot 4 inches. Standing stock still in the water and towering over me, he looked carefully over my bare body. I was dumbfounded. Not a word even entered my head. Stalemate as we remained very close and facing towards each other, he calmly said,

"Now will you go out with me?"

I was forced to admit I could see many points in his favour. However, I remained speechless. This was a perplexing moment for a nineteen year old. Suddenly, I became blessed with a superior appreciation of

Michelangelo's 'David'. Up until now this was the nearest I had been to the raw male form.

A few minutes later, without towel, he trudged through the ladies' changing room producing puddles of water in a trail behind him; like penguins exiting a pool in a zoo!

Why was I becoming so adept at attracting unwanted attention? This was the wrong guy! I was rapidly building a reputation in this field and it was one I needed to shake off. Fast.

III. November

On my way to King's Cross, I stopped at Selfridges to buy my gown for the forthcoming dinner – the highlight of my social calendar. I was not only greatly looking forward to the event, but I was also proud to be attending. It was a 'black tie' function and was often held outside the city, in a country house hotel, which added to the glamour.

I most definitely needed something spectacular to wear for the occasion. I had in mind something discreet yet sumptuous. In other words, just the sort of garment I was unlikely to be able to afford.

I found a bottle green velvet creation with no effort whatsoever. It had to be the one! As I came out of the fitting room, there was a reaction from the assistants I was hoping to duplicate on the night of the annual dinner.

"It certainly has the wow factor," said one with sincerity.

"It looks amazing on you – what a fit!" said another.

I looked in the mirror and to be perfectly honest, I had never seen myself in anything that suited me better. It really was beyond my wildest dreams. It had to be bought. It looked a million dollars. And it was, almost.

I turned over the price label slowly to lessen the pain – it represented a month's rent. Without hesitation, I decided to classify the gown as 'an investment' and only hoped that this expense could be covered by being 'grounded' for a month, or more, combined with a cheap and continuous diet of baked beans on toast for the foreseeable future!

The Boat Club was a predominantly male outfit and no one had ever seen me 'dressed to impress' so I was rather looking forward to the effect it might create.

The wobbly writing on my cheque reflected my nervous state when paying for my extravagant purchase. Now, I would most certainly not be found in a University Crew shirt and tracksuit. What a change!

I was quite confident that I would not regret what I had bought. It was exquisite. Finally, I decided 'the look' would have to be completed with junk jewellery from a charity shop. Here at least I could economise with ease.

Wearily, and to take my mind off the worry of the costly dress, I reached into my overnight bag for a textbook. Any one would do!

IV. December

We rented a spacious Victorian terraced house, its eight bedrooms covered three floors, and it was in a lovely part of the city. If the Pakistani landlord had invested in any plumbing, electrical work, painting, pointing, re-roofing and household equipment it could have been a beautiful property. It was near the Picture House, served by a useful scattering of shops, and was close to a bus route. It was even near a station!

Sadly neglected, the house was in desperate need of money spent on the fabric of the building and on interior décor, furnishings, etc. However, as individuals we paid a peppercorn weekly rent, so all in all it suited us well.

The plumbing in the house was possibly one of the worst problems; a matter of deep curiosity within the northern building trade. It was decidedly in need of updating.

The night of the much-anticipated dinner arrived. I was not to be found anywhere near the library. Instead, I was at our terraced home carefully dressing for the occasion. What ever shall I wear…?

Donning my bottle green dress, I leant over the gas fire to use the mirror. Suddenly, an unwelcome smell of scorching velvet assaulted my nasal passage, and I looked down to witness my fabulous dress slightly on fire. I banged the single flame with a nearby ruler and extinguished it instantly. No time to remedy the problem – what could one do anyway? The taxi was blowing its horn.

The taxi took me to the waiting coach outside the Student Union; at last, we were off to the country house hotel, which I knew so well.

We had the run of the entire downstairs of the place to range freely. The contrast between where we lived and rowed could not have been greater. Warmth, luxury, soft lights, antiques of all descriptions and tasteful rugs were in abundance. The public rooms all had glowing log fires – the smell from the assortment of logs was wonderful. Immediately, the surroundings evoked a feeling of relaxation and pleasure.

After quite a few drinks at the bar, on hearing the dinner gong, we wandered into the dining room. I marvelled at how smart everyone looked; the men in their black ties and dinner suits and the relatively few lady members all in full-length dresses. The table was presented in a grand and elaborate style.

A major advantage of a club dinner is that generally, the guests already know one another, which creates instant bonhomie and a great atmosphere from the start of the evening. It was a million miles away from the harsh realities of the depressed, ship-dependant city we had just left behind.

The meal consisted of many courses, featuring roast duck as the star attraction, along with plenty of wine. Port and brandy were being passed in various directions around the enormous banqueting table and speeches were about to begin. Such an intoxicating atmosphere was becoming celestial!

Dinner and speeches completed, our party drifted towards the main reception room.

There he was. Standing, glass in hand, beside the stone fireplace, talking with a handful of medics I knew, so I joined the group and soon melted into the conversation. The topic under discussion was the recent news that a woman had been chosen as leader of the Conservative Party. The guys seemed unfazed by the fact that a female should take the role. They did however question whether she would be tough enough to handle the job. Her name was Margaret Thatcher.

At least I had made a slight inroad into capturing his attention.

He had noticed me.

We had all had plenty to eat and drink and a wonderful evening's entertainment. Time to go.

Peeking out of the window looking for the coach, I noticed snow. It was sifting down like icing sugar through a sieve; the ground was covered white.

Unexpectedly, a voice behind me said,

"Can I give you a lift home? My car is outside. It's the Volkswagen Beetle."

"Yes, I know," I said.

Folding the damaged dress over to cover the scorch marks and obliterate the singeing smell at the same time, I climbed into the passenger seat, and we headed off through the snowy landscape.

"I heard about your streak," I said stupidly. "Did you make it the whole length of the road? You should have dropped in on me, for something warm afterwards."

Immediately, I regretted my blunderbuss approach. There had been no double entendre intended.

I saw him half turn his head towards me questioningly.

"I didn't mean that…that's not what I meant to say…!" I stumbled.

"Relax," he said confidently with a smile.

Prattling is not my style, so very little was said after that. The quiet seemed sufficient. It was so gratifying just to be sitting alone there with him. At last!

Sedately driving into the city, through the Haymarket and heading away from the city centre, we arrived much sooner than I had hoped at my house.

I was wallowing in the luxury of being exclusively in his company, at long last, and I didn't want it come to an end. As we parked outside, I began fervently to wish, hope against hope, that everyone in the house was either out or asleep. After all it was very late – a reasonable expectation in the circumstances.

Another concern was beginning to cross my mind – what sort of state would the place be in? Clean and tidy was extremely unlikely on a Saturday night! Empty cans of McEwan's Export and plastic containers of spicy take-away food littered around was hardly ideal. Even worse prospects filtered through my mind.

"Have a seat," I said gesturing towards the sofa. "Coffee?"

He said a black coffee would do just fine.

I closed my eyes at the appalling mess in the kitchen – the sink was overflowing with water – again! The plumbing really was a nightmare. Used pots and pans were everywhere. I wondered what he was thinking of the place. I knew he lived in Hall, where all was spick and span, cleaners, central heating, meals cooked for you. Another world!

I came back with the hot drinks. He really was a terrific looking guy – great physique, long legs, blond, really outdoorsy face and was a sensational sportsman. What more could one want?

I had never seen him in smart clothes before. He looked like a film star in his immaculate, well-tailored dinner suit. I genuinely admired his prowess at rowing and to top it all he was an engineer.

It really doesn't get any better.

All this, and the house was quiet and deserted. I couldn't have wished for more.

I sat down beside him. We had been there for several minutes when there was a cracking sound directly overhead. This was followed by creaks induced by stress. At that precise moment, a load bearing beam broke, he jumped up pulling me to one side. Water burst through the ceiling, creating an avalanche of plaster, wooden slats, more water, and dust. We now both looked like workers from the nearby Spillers Flour Mill! The dust was everywhere. The fall continued with gaps in between for a couple of minutes. There was nothing one could do to stop it.

The rubble covered the carpet, the table, and chairs, and sofa were all lost in the aftermath. The pile of debris was above waist height in parts and effectively divided the room into two distinct halves.

He was on one side of the mountain. I was on the other.

This event rather dampened the atmosphere, in more ways than one!

A steady water trickle was gaining momentum down the side of the wall, and onto the mass of plasterwork beneath, beginning to make it into a solid mass.

I wanted to pretend nothing had happened and just carry on. Speaking had become an impossibility due to the levels of dust in the confined space.

As he turned away, a final lump of white dust-covered masonry landed on the shoulder of his dinner jacket. Bullseye! This was too much to bear – the last straw. I had reached my Tipping Point, thirty-eight degrees.

What a debacle!

Ignoring his offer of help, I replied flatly, "Goodnight." It was all I could manage in the circumstances.

On his way out, he turned as he left the room and called out: "By the way you look much better in shorts and wellies!"

His eyes travelled down my burned dress, where I was standing covered in white dust, surrounded by masonry. The Blitz Spirit was required to carry this off with aplomb I felt.

Lastly, he added with a smile, "See you at the boathouse on Wednesday." And my heart soared.

I experienced a strange blend of happiness and sadness. Sad that the wonderful evening, which had held such promise for the future, had literally ended in tatters. Happy that he had confirmed our next meeting date. I supressed a near overwhelming urge to cry with frustration. Instead, I peered fiercely down at my dress and kicked the full skirt with venom with my shoe, as if it were in some way to blame for wrecking the last few minutes of the otherwise perfect evening. On hearing the front door shut, and a car engine start, my heart sank.

Turning to more practical matters, I now had to consider how to get out of this mess and up the stairs to bed. Crossing the mound of rubble was simply not possible. I would be pleased to see the miniature crossed wooden oars, which were displayed on the outside of my bedroom door, tonight! I felt drained, but not sleepy; I needed some rest.

The only route I could take was to leave by the kitchen door, through the backyard, onto the alley. As I approached the front door via the road to enter the house, I saw fresh car tyre marks in the snow where we had parked. His parking spot now empty.

I came inside quietly and climbed the stairs, avoiding treading on the hateful dress as I did so. Walking past the landing window towards my bedroom door there was something in the corridor, right outside my room. I could not make it out in the half-light, what could it be? As I neared the object, I thought I detected a soft whistling in the background. I stopped to listen but heard nothing. Bending down to retrieve the unknown item, I hesitated. Then I beamed a huge grin. It was a large black pair of men's wellington boots!

The Dragons of Bethenhurst

It wasn't a particularly attractive Kentish village. In fact, it was quite the reverse really. In its favour was a group of oast houses; additionally, the church contained several examples of Burne-Jones' work in the form of stained-glass windows. Pre-Raphaelite glasswork was the only artistically noteworthy aspect of the entire community. These gems had undoubtedly gone largely unnoticed by most residents, except the odd local dilettantes.

All in all, it was quite a dull place to live. Nothing ever happened.

It had become popular as a place to make a home for sheerly practical reasons; the nearby station had fast links to London and there were an assortment of 'good schools' in the locality. Just the sort of information estate agents liked to hear, indeed, they judged the place to be a lucrative hunting ground. Hence, house prices had escalated.

In summary, the territory had become overpriced and remained unexceptional. For many, transport and schools seemed the key reasons Bethenhurst continued to exist.

Some distance from the centre of the village, the Post Office was situated. This nondescript roadside facility was, by and large, the only amenity used by the inhabitants. Bethenhurst also afforded a local pub patriotically named 'The George and Dragon'. This was now only frequented by outsiders who could accept its crazy prices. These weekend, visitors filled the pub's carpark with a wide range of Porsches and BMWs. The vehicles were proudly displayed in neat rows to the front of the pub, thereby denoting the status of the hostelry. The remainder of the week, both the venue and its carpark were deserted!

The Post Office in question also contained groceries and other essential items inevitably found in small rural shops. The combined shop and Post Office was run by a husband and wife team, who were desperate to sell the loss-making venture.

Two years ago, they had bought the business as a form of semi-retirement. It had lost money from the very start. Despite all their efforts, they were quite unable to sell the premises, which also contained their living quarters.

Amazingly, they always managed to seem cheerful and helpful despite being trapped in a loss-making business and home. To make matters financially worse, their twin daughters had both received offers from London University medical schools, to read for five-year medical degree courses, which they had accepted!

The Post Office had focal-point status in the community. Despite pensions now being paid directly into bank accounts (thereby negating the need to visit the establishment to collect pension payments), the elderly continued to regularly visit the Post Office; principally for social contact.

They would congregate noisily, like birds massing pre-migration, around the small counter area. The counter was utilised in the way 'propping up the bar' in the pub was favoured in earlier times. Very few postal transactions ever took place! It became the norm for the Post Office to be thronged with chattering, non-paying, elderly folk masquerading as customers. This was particularly noticeable on chilly days, as the Post Office was always kept at a sweltering temperature; it made a cosy alternative to a chat at home.

On this particular spring day, the Post Office was scorchingly hot, as the sun shone benevolently over the entire village. The weather afforded the opportunity to keep the shop door propped open with a cast iron boot scraper. At the time, there appeared to be nobody in the shop besides Mary, the relief counter assistant, who was busy phoning through the bakery order for delivery.

Unbeknown, one surprisingly tall (for his age) pensioner was lurking amongst the vegetables on display. He was rummaging through the boxes of vegetables and muttering that they were not up to his standard.

George, 92, had given up his allotment as it had become too much for him to cope with, and now had to rely on the ageing and miserable selection of root vegetables in the shop. Meanwhile a van drew up outside the building. No one took any notice. The driver left the engine running and headed towards the village shop. He was dressed in black.

George, who was by now bent double in his relentless investigation of the vegetable boxes on the floor, had his head down, giving the task his undivided attention. Sighing with backache from bending, he resorted to kneeling behind the shelves of bread and pastries in his quest to find the perfect carrot.

The newest entrant to this bucolic scene moved straight towards the open counter of the Post Office. When the assistant looked up, he was holding a gun pointed directly at her face. She let out a strangled gasp as she took stock of the situation.

"Shut up!" shouted the gunman. "Keep quiet, and empty the till."

Mary trembled as her eyes fixed on the handgun, which was unbelievably close to her head. Her first thought was, *What have I done to deserve this?* Her body felt stiff with fear; she tried to move but could not. Despite her state of mind, one detail caught Mary's attention.

The small emblem on the man's lapel. A dragon.

"Give me the money!" rasped the man in black.

At this moment, George, who had incidentally given up finding any even half-decent carrots, discovered what he judged to be a worthy savoy cabbage in the adjacent box. Aha! Persistence does pay off. This should keep me going for at least a week. He mulled over the prospect with relish.

Content with this 'find', George began to rise from his uncomfortable position on all fours. As he did so, he popped the vast vegetable into the strong plastic bag he was holding. What a weight! Noiselessly and gradually, he rose to his feet.

Despite his age, he was still a remarkable six foot three in height, and the last few inches required him to lever himself upwards by use of the bakery shelves.

Finally, he became vertical.

He gazed across the shop to regain his bearings, after such a prolonged period on the floor he was feeling a little giddy! Suddenly, his pale eyes alighted on the hand-held gun pointed straight at Mary. He assessed the situation in an instant. Clearly, he was no fool and his old eyes had not deceived him in 92 years.

The confrontation at the Post Office counter seemed frozen in time. Mary remained static, unable to move a single muscle, and the gunman could not reach his goal without her cooperation.

Deadlock.

Wide-eyed Mary looked towards George as he surfaced. He emerged viciously whirling the bag containing the massive cabbage above his head; advancing, he wore the expression of one demented upon his face. His improvised revolving vegetable weapon seemed to have the power of the main rotor blade of a Chinook helicopter, as it circled ever harder and faster above George's head!

George came up behind the man, who was still pointing the firearm at Mary. As the gunman turned towards George, the bagged cabbage hit him resoundingly on the temple. Blood began to seep from his ear. The gun fell to the floor, skidded across the lino and stopped at George's feet. Deftly, he retrieved the weapon whereupon Mary flew from behind the counter, through the internal door and disappeared.

George, now in possession of the gun, was about to tackle the robber when the latter stumbled to his feet. Holding his head in his hands, he staggered through the open door and outside. Passing his vehicle, he attempted his escape on foot!

George shouted, "Ring the police! He can't go far in that condition," just as the owners of the shop came rushing down the stairs and onto the scene of the crime.

As the afternoon wore on, despite a few reporters outside the premises, everything seemed back to normal in Bethenhurst.

By 5:30, that afternoon the gunman had been apprehended and was held in police custody.

Until 5:30, the village shop remained open, as usual.

Just after 5:30, George sat down at his table; he felt he deserved his plate filled with mince and mash, accompanied by a generous helping of savoy cabbage. Dallying over the events of the day, he allowed himself the indulgence of a little self-congratulatory smile.

'Bethenhurst was such a dull village. Nothing ever happened'—a view so often expressed.

These words were floating around George's brain until a soft thud announced the arrival of the local paper on the hall mat. Stooping to collect the newspaper, his attention was drawn to the thrilling headline news:

George the Dragon Slayer
Bethenhurst hero battles gunman with cabbage...

In all the years he had lived in Bethenhurst, there had never been so much excitement, and in all probability there never would be again, he reasoned. "Well," George added aloud and with finality, "Definitely not in my lifetime!"

He paused, began to laugh and continued to laugh. He then continued to laugh for quite some time.

In essence, my tale is complete.

Later events prompted me to extend the story, thereby closing the loop.

Addendum

All good things come to an end, and George was no exception. At his funeral service, a poem was chosen by his grandchildren, a verse being read by each child.

"Memories"
The love we have for Grandad
Will never fade away.
We'll think of him, our special friend,
Throughout each passing day.

We'll walk into a room
And see his empty chair,
Although we know he's resting,
We'll feel his presence there.

The memories of his laughter,
His warm and loving smile,
His eyes so full of happiness,
His heart, that of a child.

Memories are forever,
Be they laughter or of tears,
Memories we will treasure,
Through all the coming years.

My tribute to George, his ingenuity and courage was by reading aloud 'The Dragons of Bethenhurst'.

The order of service sheet was in my hand, as returning to my pew, I noted the lines:

'The family invites you all to join them for refreshments at the George and Dragon, Bethenhurst, after the service.'

Was this ironic choice of venue a nod to George's heroism, or just convenience? Either way, it would certainly have given George the last laugh. That would really have appealed to him. Right down to the ground!

Sky High

A great company, a great placement, and great for my C.V. This was to be the second industrial placement of my postgraduate course. Having been lucky enough to secure I.C.I North Tees, on the oil cracking plant in the first instance, I imagined that would be hard to top. A second placement of that calibre at Rolls Royce Aero Engines Division seemed too good to be true. It also came with a sense of déjà-vu, as my father, a former Spitfire pilot, had been a test pilot based there after the war. History repeating itself.

The only drawback was as this was unpaid; I needed a part time job to help cover the double rent I would now be paying. It would have to be close to my digs and workplace, as I had no transport at this point in my career. No money for luxuries. No money for essentials, come to think of it!

I had spotted a hotel, part of a large group, near the M4. Hotels always needed staff and this was a large organisation, part of a chain. When I arrived, I earmarked this as ideally situated. I could walk there and back home after work easily. Ideal.

After an interview lasting less than two minutes with the Executive Head Chef, the key question was asked:

"What size bust are you?"

I was a little taken aback by this seemingly irrelevant enquiry and paused before answering,

"Thirty-four inches." I felt like asking, why do you need to know that? However, I needed a job, so I kept the last comment to myself.

He smiled, evidently relieved by my answer and continued,

"We haven't any overalls for forty inches or above. You'll do alright." Adding, "You'll fit in nicely."

I dutifully laughed at his little joke.

"That's sorted," he concluded, banging down his hand on a mound of unopened mail on his desk. "Start at seven tonight!"

"What am I employed to do?" I asked enthusiastically.

"Night shift kitchen cleaner," was his daunting response.

Life in the kitchen wasn't too bad. Particularly, when I was asked to do overtime, as I then qualified for a staff meal. Part-timers and casuals are usually given all the rotten jobs. Mine was effectively a rotten job already so I had nothing to fear; logically, extra tasks could only get better I figured!

The hotel was really busy. Some evenings we catered for four hundred covers on banqueting alone, apart from the normal dining room guest meals. Everything from weddings to First Division Footballers' pre-match high teas were all concocted in the hotel kitchen. There was never any shortage of work to be completed.

My last task of the evening was when the conveyor belt dishwasher, stacked high with crates of glasses one on top of the other, plates, dishes, etc., was turned off. The drum had to be entered to clean out all the accumulated debris that had collected inside during the course of the evening. Retrieving bits of bone, forks caught up in the mesh, plasters, etc. was my least preferred task. The steam and heat alone were bad enough. It wasn't a job for the hair-conscious female!

Turnaround time on the wash up team was enormously quick. Loading and unloading manually proved to be a constant frantic race to keep up with the machine. Handling the clean boiling hot plates and other items stacked upright on the giant machine caused real problems for the skin, which bubbled up under the surface with such constant exposure to heat. At least there was none of the usual low-key conversations to endure from my fellow workers, as the noise level was deafening.

Kitchen work is largely routine and monotonous. It is also hard and dirty and hot. As you are not 'front of the house', you never see a customer, only the other staff. I was only going to be employed there for a few months, but I had heartfelt sympathy for those who would remain after I headed north. Periodically, Vincent the Head Chef, who had engaged me, tried to persuade me into lunchtime work as a waitress. This I was unable to help with as I was actively engaged at the engineering company, which had to come first as it was my raison d'être.

"What a shame," he said when I had to turn him down. "You are so presentable," I was flattered until he added, "for a student."

As my shift came to an end, each of the five nights of the week I worked, Henry the sole overnight member of staff, who tended to the kitchen when there were no meals being prepared, emerged from the shadows like a beast from its lair! His shift occasionally slightly overlapped with mine. Henry had a unique status among the staff. He was respected, always addressed in a cheerful fashion, and revered. He worked in the kitchen as an overnight caretaker (I never really knew what his job entailed, but I felt there was not a job description attached to Henry's role. Henry always worked alone).

Henry was short, solidly built, with a severely chiselled face. His strong lower jaw gave him a primeval appearance. He had the look of one not easily swayed to change his mind. He moved like grease lightening when removing the pig bins and other similar heavy tasks. He was a shining example of toughness and durability, always exhibiting a workmanlike approach to doing whatever he was tasked to do. Both, his body and his attitude were designed for work.

Whenever there were any decent leftovers from the dining room, a half-eaten steak, half a carafe of wine (we were not allowed to drink any alcohol whilst on duty in the kitchen) they were relentlessly put aside on a shelf for Henry. Even the most uncharitable kitchen porter found something for Henry. He was like an old much loved family Labrador. The kitchen provided both his family and his home.

I was determined to get to the bottom of his mysterious employment and existence. It was fascinating. Nobody ever talked about Henry. The only information freely available was that he was Polish. I had never even heard Henry speak.

Perhaps his English wasn't too good I wondered. Nobody enlightened me. Perhaps no one talked to him because he looked so tough and fierce. He was just here to do the job – and that was all that mattered. Everyone left him alone to do it. I resolved when next I saw Henry to strike up a conversation.

One Saturday evening, I was asked to do an extra hour, which was always welcome news; as not only extra pay but a meal too would be available. Henry was just starting his overnight shift by cleaning out the fat from the frying equipment. Now was my chance. As I began to speak to him, Alan, one of the chefs looked up in alarm. The next minute he was hovering defensively next to Henry.

"Hello, Henry! Had a good day so far?" I ventured.

Henry just stood there looking straight through me with his dark eyes expressionless – like stones. I smiled to encourage him, and began speaking to him again.

He stared at me uncomprehendingly with a deadpan look on his face.

The chef intervened and said,

"He won't reply."

"Why? Is his English non-existent?" I said questioningly.

"No," he said firmly. "The Nazis cut his tongue out. That was about the nicest thing that they did to him by all accounts."

It was at that point I saw the telltale numbers branded on his wrist. I felt humbled. Wiser but sadder I went back to my work.

My one foray into waitressing ended rather unexpectedly. Vincent had asked if I would be prepared to waitress for a small function to be held in a private room. This was an evening slot. A respectable all-male golf club affair. Downing my divided double bucket and donning a waitress uniform (size 34!) I thought this would make a change for the better; at least I could dispense with the overalls for one evening!

The party were well-inebriated it would be fair to say, and as I had both hands full of hot plated food I bent over the table to serve the dishes. I felt something tickle the back of my neck and in a trice my zip was unfastened by someone behind me.

Trapped between the chairs either side of me and the trolley behind me, I bumped the plates down abruptly on the table, to find the uniform dress had slipped off my shoulders down to my waist.

There I was half undressed – the only person standing up! Amid raucous calls and hoots, I left the room and resumed my former role with the bucket.

At least one point had become clear to me – why Vincent had been so anxious to have a good fit in my work wear. It was not prompted by his sense of haute couture. One size bigger and the dress would have fallen off me completely!

The flushed colour to my cheeks must have given me away. When I returned to the kitchen, everyone was laughing. They had a rough idea of what would happen. Apparently, Vincent chose his waitresses based on their handling of this acid test. The golfers were a renowned bunch. I am led to believe they were even more badly behaved at Christmas. I made a mental note of this for the future!

Weekends during the shooting season was when I came into my own. I could get out in the fresh air and enjoy life. Currently, I had no dog, so I was unable to be a picker-up of lost or wounded birds, but I enjoyed being part of the beating team. It was a beautiful estate, with lakes for duck shooting and plenty of woodland cover for pheasants, which were reared in large numbers. The guest list of guns read like a copy of 'Who's Who'. Cabinet Ministers to industrialists and aristocrats were present. It made a welcome contrast to my evening job.

His Lordship sometimes handed his gun to the keeper to shoot, and joined the beating line. He was always keen to hear about life outside his estate. He was obviously moved by the episode involving Henry. However, he didn't seem amused when I regaled my tale of the 'undress' at the golfers' dinner. I suppose he did not have many opportunities to sample life as an employee and workplace humour can be an acquired taste!

I explained to him how the large-scale theft of sides of beef had been carried out during the evening shift, right under our noses, with nearly one hundred kitchen staff present, and no one noticing!

I began to regret this as he pulled out a notebook from his shooting jacket pocket and began jotting down the details. He then shook my hand and turned to join his guests before saying to me,

"As chairman of the Brewery in question and a principal share-holder, your information is most valuable."

I had to laugh, albeit somewhat later in the day! He must have been virtually the only person in the country not to have told this kitchen tale to. Now, only I could have managed that!

My two jobs were beginning to take their toll – maybe I should start investing in some anti-ageing cream I surmised. The work at the estate was really paid fun rather than income driven, but I was more than a little worried about His Lordship's reaction to my diverting stories of 'Life in the Kitchen: a microcosm of life' as I had rather grandly described it. Might they have further repercussions? I wondered if anti-anxiety cream was also available at the chemists.

Most evenings, despite the hotel providing minibus transport for workers, I walked back. This was brought about by the time-tabling of the late night staff buses. I was always unable to be transported on the hour, so rather than wait a full sixty minutes for the next scheduled bus it was quicker to walk to my digs. However tired I felt, the fresh air the walk afforded was always welcome. My female colleagues termed me as 'crazy'.

It was not a great walk, especially at that time of night, or indeed the early hours of the morning. The first part involved a ten-minute trot down a secluded lane; there were high hedges on both sides. The sheep dozing on the other side were often disturbed by my footfall and would catapult up bleating with indignation, as their beauty sleep was rudely interrupted! Their sudden movement never failed to make me jump. Often a fox would dart out of the undergrowth; it seemed strange, so near the city and motorway, to be in a semi-rural landscape.

I passed a small farmhouse that was always in darkness by the time I was trudging home, my thoughts solely on getting to bed. As usual, the muffled sound of a sheepdog barking from within a barn greeted me. I felt rather guilty about disturbing so many creatures five nights a week!

Halfway along the lane, I became aware of a vehicle behind me. It must have pulled out of the staff car park and was creeping slowly along the lane. The headlights were on main beam, and as I walked along, the long shadow from my body was cast onto the road surface ahead. I did not want to turn around and face the car. Perhaps it was an over-cautious driver, who did not want to be stopped and breathalysed. I determined to keep a steady, even pace and not to panic. I tried to remember the whereabouts of the next gate, as the height of the hedges made any necessary deviation, right or left, a virtual impossibility.

All the while, I kept telling myself I had backpacked round the world single-handed; I had acquired many of the skills of self-preservation, in a variety of character forming experiences, early on in my life. The often quoted 'Keep Calm and Carry On' seemed to be the universal message in so many circumstances in life. Strange to relate, my mind began to focus on Henry. Now there was someone who could handle whatever life threw at him.

The vehicle was gaining on me. There was no doubt about that. There was hardly sufficient room for it to pull alongside me. But that is what it did. I imagined my walking in the dead of night a regular beat, near a hotel, had attracted a kerb-crawler? Was he going to pull me into the car…?

Involuntarily my head turned and I saw a white Ford Granada, with a bright red strip around the middle. It was a jam butty car! A smile of relief passed over my lips as two uniformed officers came into view. The driver rolled down the window. I was about to say,

"Have you got a light, guv?" but when I saw the expression he was wearing, I thought better of this!

"What are you doing?" was his first remark.

"Going home from work at the hotel," I replied.

"Yes, we know," was his rejoinder. "Get in the car."

It transpired they had me under surveillance for some time. There had been an attempted murder of a woman in the lane some months ago.

Apparently, I had become their 'decoy', and they were grateful for the fact I was unwittingly 'helping them with their enquiries'.

"We will give you a lift back to your digs," he offered.

"Get the staff bus tomorrow," added his colleague.

"I don't want to see you again," said the first officer as I was returned home. "Dead or alive," he added as a point of clarification.

The staff Christmas party was to be held in early January on weekdays when we were least busy. Mondays and Tuesdays were the days chosen as obviously not everyone could attend at once – someone had to man the job!

The theme of the fancy dress was to be Nursery Rhymes and Children. I had little time at my disposal for creative sewing and needlework so I was forced to hire my outfit from a theatrical costumier in Bath.

Paddy McPherson, my landlady's son, was to be my guest. Most staff were very hush-hush about their costumes, so I amused myself thinking of a ballroom containing two hundred Bo Peeps. I had chosen my outfit with care; past experience had taught me wearing an elaborate historical outfit can be uncomfortably hot and can prove very impractical at the same time!

Clearly, Paddy's offer of driving us to the hotel was the best bet. He emerged as a very credible Charlie Chaplin, and managed to look at home in his costume. I had chosen a gymslip with black stockings and suspenders, schoolgirl panama and satchel and carried my hockey stick, along with the 'Swot Book of Arithmetic'. I thought we looked a winning combination for the prize on offer – if a little sombre in colour.

Dancing was to a live band, and the ballroom was crowded. Often it was hard to detect who it was beneath their elaborate guise. One brave soul dressed as 'Hickory Dickory Dock' was trying to walk in a large papier-mâché clock case! The face of the clock was behind his head, which was encased in a box. Every time he wanted to speak or sip a drink, he had to ask someone to open the polythene covered box door with a latch that opened on the outside. I never did find out whom it was inside!

My favourite costume was possibly the simplest. Some inventive individual had sewn two sheepskins roughly together with leather laces. The Neanderthal was sandwiched in between the skins, and had a necklace made from small bones. He carried a huge leg bone as a cudgel – presumably from the kitchen!

At the end of the evening, I stayed behind with a few others to help in the clearing up operation. It was not far off dawn when Paddy and I returned to the Ford Escort, which by this time stood more or less alone in the staff car park. It had been a bitterly cold night, and a deep frost covered the ground. He tried to get the key in the lock on each door in turn, but to no avail. We were locked out of the car, well and truly!

"Let's walk back," said Paddy. "It's not that far, twenty minutes at most."

I was just about to explain to him why I didn't think that was one of his better ideas, when he grabbed my arm and we started off.

The reader at this point could be forgiven for trying to guess the ending of my tale. Believe me you almost certainly will not.

It was now that dawn broke, in the grey light straight ahead of me, I was horrified at what I saw.

A flock of thirty to forty sheep were filing out of the field through a gap in the hedge. The majority were just standing on the road. The others were heading directly towards the M4. Trying to push the sheep on the road back through the hole in the hedge proved an impossibility. The moment you turned them round they scattered, right and left, further up or down the lane! The stragglers nearest the motorway were the biggest risk, so Paddy and I tried to turn them and hold them on the road.

I looked up towards the nearby farmhouse. Thank God! There were some lights on. I prayed the farmer would come out to count his stock before breakfast, with his sheepdog. My prayers were partly rewarded. He arrived on foot, but with no dog.

"We need a dog to hold the sheep!" I shouted. "Bring the dog – now!"

"I'll try and bunch the stragglers," Paddy called helpfully.

"Right enough," said the owner of the sheep.

The farmer appeared to be moving in slow motion as he walked back towards the steading. We needed the dog quickly. There were too many in the flock for us to hold stationary much longer and they would start breaking out all over the place. All hell would be let loose.

He came back to my relief, but not with a crook or a dog. He was carrying a camera! All I needed now was that patrol car containing the two officers to bowl up…

Their timing was spot on. In my peripheral vision, I could see, advancing along the lane, a white Ford Granada flashing its red beacon light, guaranteed to unnerve the already testy sheep. They were bound to bolt.

Quickly the officers assessed the situation and joined in our efforts to contain the sheep to stop them leaking out onto the motorway.

"Where's the damned farmer?" said Paddy with a mixture of exasperation and sweat covering his face. "They're his sheep! He's the only one not helping!"

It was a sentiment shared by all present. Frankly, any one of the Bo Peeps at the party would have been more useful than the farmer. At least they were all well-armed with crooks!

Slowly, but surely the sheep were filing back into the field, as gingerly the four of us gently moved forward, herding the animals very slowly. I was bending down with my arms cupped, a revealing aspect in a gymslip, one of the policemen had slipped on the droppings on the road and was lying there next to his hat, Charlie Chaplin was standing next to the Panda car, waving his arms in the air. It was an action-packed picture.

Just at that moment, I heard a camera shutter click. It was the farmer. He was standing by a gate, camera in hand. He had just opened the gate to let in the sheep!

Calmly and with great dignity, the sheep proceeded in an orderly fashion, as if they were practising for entering a show ring of a prestigious stock judging competition. Without cajoling from any corner, they dutifully trotted along the lane towards the open gate and returned to their grazing pasture.

The sheepdog continued his lie-in, and never made an appearance on the scene.

The upright policeman stared at me muttering,

"I had a feeling this would have something to do with you."

This I hoped was the end of the episode. Unfortunately, I was proved wrong. The farmer duly entered his photograph in the local paper competition. The title of this competition was 'An Amusing Scene with Animals'.

The press responsible for publishing the paper had other ideas, or so it seemed. When I saw the front-page photograph and the leading article on my desk at work, I could not believe my eyes. There I was, pictured in a short gymslip, bending down, facing the camera with two policemen and Charlie Chaplin surrounded by a flock of alarmed sheep.

It was captioned, 'Sky High: Fun and Games at Jolity Farm'. I was not looking forward to the rest of Monday morning in the office.

Having to account for the escapade at some point seemed inevitable. My only consolation was that the story was so fantastic and incredible; it just had to be true. I was banking on this principal. It was the only defence I could muster.

Vanuatu 1982

Sold the house, furniture into storage, disposed of the car, and lastly the ultimate sacrifice – handed in my notice. It felt as if I had jumped off a cliff.

Drastic measures indeed. My life needed a re-vamp; having discarded all the trappings I was foot-loose and fancy free, finally! Backpack at the ready, I was headed towards Heathrow grasping my precious round the world flight ticket. Pre-booked and pre-paid it represented my future life, in one small folding ticket book.

I had read Sir Arthur Grimble's 'Pattern of Islands' as a thirteen-year-old, and had decided the Gilbert and Ellice isles were places I just had to visit. Now was the right time. Well, it was now or never really. I should point out the term 'back packing' had only recently been coined and travelling the globe was not a regular or accepted rite of passage for young people. At this time, it most decidedly was not the norm. It was thirteen years since I had read the book and much had changed, including the names of the islands. Now they are identified as Kiribati (Gilberts) and Tuvalu (Ellice) isles on the map. However, if I could find a supply vessel working its way around any of the islands of Melanesia, this would be perfect. I acknowledged a copra steamer might not be so easily accessible these days! This was a concession I would have to be prepared to make, despite wanting to re-enact the autobiographical travelogue by Grimble.

Several months of travelling had brought me to the large island of New Caledonia in the South Pacific, where I spent three expensive weeks. As I left Noumea Airport, via the tiny aircraft provided by Air Nauru I was able to see many of the eighty-two islands, known before independence as the New

Hebrides and currently as Vanuatu, which forms an archipelago.

Flying at low level gave an ideal overview of the pattern of islands for which I had come so far to experience.

My bed and breakfast provider was a local taxi driver. Yves, the other guest was French; together we hired a car to visit the key spots on the main island of Vanuatu called Efate. The whole island was able to be circumnavigated, by road, easily in a day.

Some of the smaller islands were mere sandy ribbons poking out of the warm shallow waters. Local residents would haul up their skirts and literally walk from one island to another island.

Currently, a selection of tiny outcrops was being visited by staff of the Bank of England, who was endeavouring to encourage the islanders to use Vatu, the official currency. Apparently, each time the bankers disappeared, the locals would bury the money in the sand, and go back to using their own particular store of wealth – seashells!

Yves and I visited the local market in the capital, Port Vila, which was the only real town. We were amused to see all the prices being marked up. Clothes, fruits, even hotels and restaurants were upping their menu prices. One might well ask why? An Australian cruise ship was due to visit Port Vila later that day, obviously the market traders, et al. were forewarned and forearmed!

We returned to our digs with coconut crab bought at the market, which we cooked over charcoal. It was a meal to remember.

I was keen to start my adventure at sea, before I lost my nerve. The Burns Philp shipping quay was my first port of call, as the base was principally used by the type of vessel I was looking to board.

I approached a battered looking craft named Onmar II, berthed nearby, and explained to the skipper in a mixture of English, French and sign language where I wanted to go. The answer was not negotiable, as it was too late in the year to visit these islands as I had planned. It was now the cyclone season in that part of the Pacific. Consequently, there would be no small boats on the route for several weeks. This was not what I wanted to hear, having travelled nearly eleven thousand miles to explore the area.

All was not lost, or so it seemed, as the skipper was leaving tomorrow on a round trip to several of the islands of Vanuatu, stopping further south at the island of Tanna. Then heading northwards to Ambrym, Pentecost, and Espiritu Santo. There I could disembark or could take the return journey directly back to Port Vila.

We discussed a few details. I needed to bring my own food and drink. There were no cabins for passengers. Those islanders, who were to stay overnight on the vessel, slept on plaited palm mats they brought with them, in the open air on the deck. It was likely to be a Spartan few days.

I trusted the skipper, but the youthful crew were eyeing me with interest and disbelief that a young white woman would want to undertake this journey alone.

I had mentioned my proposed trip to several people I had met in Port Vila – just to make sure, if I never returned they would know where to start looking for me! Their unanimous view was that this venture was fraught with danger and risky in the extreme. I would have to be insane to undertake the voyage.

It was too late to change my mind. I had come so far; I was determined to go through with the journey of a lifetime.

I watched as we loaded our cargo from the quayside to the hold, everything was moved by hand and hand barrows, even the bags of cement. I began to draw a parallel with the 'puffer' steamers that were such a lifeline along the West Coast of Scotland extending as far as the Inner and Outer Hebrides. Everything from coal, barrels of herring to whisky and post were carried by this mode of transport in times gone by. I had to smile when I found out that Onmar II had been built in Buckie, not thirty miles from the home and job I had left behind!

The hold was nowhere near full as we were bound to load and reload on our voyage. The cargo of little piglets being transported were running around loose in the hold. More disturbingly, two people described as lunatics were bound at their ankles and wrists and were also kept in the hold. The toilet was a single shared bucket, which we took turns to empty via a rope dangled over the side of the boat and then trawled through the water.

The first time I saw a group of sharks, at least their dorsal fins, surrounding the vessel, I dropped the rope by accident, and thereby made myself thoroughly unpopular.

When I awoke the first morning, my eyes were greeted by an amazing sight. The sea was flat-calm like a sheet of glass. Looming straight out of the Pacific Ocean was a smoking gunmetal grey mound. Surrounded by the silver grey light of early dawn, pearly clouds and a hint of sea mist; it formed a symphony in subtle greys. This monochrome palette formed a tonal picture I will never forget. It was the backcloth for the volcano Yasur.

Within a couple of hours, the sea state and other conditions took a turn for the worse. I joined the skipper in the wheel house. Beads of sweat were evident across his brow and he looked troubled.

Blithely, I asked, "Is there an Onmar I?"

His reply was gesticulating, by use of the international sign language, using the thumbs down signal.

"On the reef. Here!" he added for my edification. I quickly decided not to interrupt with banal conversation again.

"Missy, go below," he snapped. "Take my cabin. Lie down."

I obeyed without question. I remained there for the next three days.

The cabin, the size of a cupboard, had a bed like a large drawer, basically a mattress with wooden sides. If I lay spread eagle, my hands and feet could touch the wooden panels, which formed the perimeter walls. By this method, I kept horizontal and stable. I lay in this position as the wind grew in strength and the waves repeatedly hit the glass window. It shattered into fragments. If you raised your head, it would immediately thump into the sidewalls. The roaring of the sea and wind outside was petrifying. The bed was soaked with seawater.

Diesel fumes and the constant rolling motion formed a toxic mix. The recurring feeling of wanting to vomit, but with no food or drink able to be prepared or consumed, this was not clinically possible.

There was absolutely no let up.

The physical feeling was akin to being hideously drunk. An ever-present sensation of your head going backwards, as you lay down. Trying to fight the predicament was an ongoing challenge, it was a struggle for survival.

The conditions were so dire, Turner's seascapes were brought to mind, and I wondered how he endured the torture of being tied to the mast, to observe and record his experiences on canvas.

Moving away from the negative side of the situation, I tried to focus on the positive aspects.

Strangely, despite the lack of food and drink, these items did not feature in my 'think positive' regime. Dispensing with the continuous throb of the engine and the torrent of vile smelling diesel. Being able to wash. Dry clothes and bedding. Land beneath my feet. I disciplined myself to concentrate on these motivating factors, and keep hope firmly on my horizon.

It was hard to avoid the reality that I could not read, or write my diary, due to the weather state, despite having plenty of time at my disposal. I hated to admit this, but there was a voice inside that whispered, why keep a diary – when you know you will never return? There were occasional points where I was convinced I would die.

'Returning' was my new buzzword. Getting back to land and off this floating hell. Return I must…

Eventually, we moored at Espiritu Santo, it seemed deserted. There had been no supply vessels for several weeks, so the few shops had empty shelves and had not bothered to open. They had nothing to sell.

I walked to the water's edge to swim and wash, when a passer-by warned me that because the US troop ship 'President Coolidge' sank at that spot, sharks habitually fed there. So no wash for me!

The place echoed mood indigo; deserted Nissen huts from World War II and grizzly lumps of rusting military equipment. It felt as if the Americans had only just left.

I called into a café and asked for scrambled eggs, but as there was no milk to be had anywhere on the island, this straightforward request could not be granted.

I decided there and then, I would take the return passage aboard Onmar II.

The direct route back to our port of origin seemed quite tame compared to the trauma of the outward-bound passage. Now we were not too far from land, and although the Burns Philp shipping quay was nowhere in sight, the skipper allowed the crew to go below and use the galley. I shared with the crew, a meal of boiled rice with thin strips of boiled cabbage on top. Believe me, no delicacy ever tasted so good! The relief and change of mood from the deck hands to the skipper, was infectious and a joy to behold. They all appeared relaxed and happy in their work. My prayers were about to be answered imminently; I could see land. I would soon be getting off this old tub, and sleep the whole night through in a comfortable bed, and on dry land. I could not wait.

After the meal in the galley, I lay down on the padded bench seat that surrounded the table.

I had the biggest headache in the Southern Hemisphere. Nevertheless, I fell straight into the deepest sleep of my life. The sleep of exhaustion.

I awoke briefly in the fading light of early evening, and the skipper told me not to disembark until the cargo was unloaded for safety's sake. *Fine*, I thought, we have made it back, which was the overriding factor. I reclined again on my makeshift bed. I had a smile on my face of pleasure and contentment. I could relax now and despite my headache, I drifted back into sleep. After all we had endured, a good rest was called for, and was long overdue.

It is difficult to estimate the length of time I slept in total. Awakening for the second time, I sat up on my bench-cum-bed and looked around. I was still in a soporific state when I turned and glanced over my shoulder into the darkness. Dimly on the horizon behind me, I saw lights.

It was then I heard the familiar insistent sound of a marine engine, and my senses became acutely aware of the pervasive smell of diesel. All at once I was fully awake. In a nightmarish moment of panic, I let out a howl, fit to accompany Edvard Munch's *'The Scream'*. It echoed around in my head and was most probably able to be heard in the Alps. Not just the Southern Alps, the Swiss ones as well!

The lights fading into the distance behind were the harbour lights of Port Vila.

We were headed out to sea.

My emotions ran riot. I could not decide whether to laugh or cry, so I tried both simultaneously! True enough, my journey of a lifetime had proved a character forming experience. But once in a lifetime was more than sufficient!

Strange to Relate

The estate's reputation was principally based on the rare and ancient Caledonian Pine Forest, the remnants of which were sufficient to support a reasonable sized population of capercaillie. In addition, there was good salmon fishing on the Tanar, deerstalking and a grouse moor besides. Given its position, not too far from Aberdeen, I made regular trips inland to ride in its glens.

Spring heralded the bright yellow coconut smelling gorse to enliven the landscape, followed by veins of purple heather spreading alongside the main artery of the river and beyond. The soft-topped green hills framed the scene, which had captivated Queen Victoria, and attracted and entranced followers ever since.

Arguably, it afforded the best, varied, and scenic riding in Aberdeenshire. Certainly, it was hard to beat.

The layout of the stables consisted of a single storey courtyard. Housed within the central square were several fudge coloured Norwegian Fjord ponies. A tough and hardy breed, they stood outside tethered to metal rings embedded in the stonewall. They seemed content to stand there in all weathers, just munching on their hay bags. They tolerated, with good grace, the occasional interruption to their routine, when they were expected to ride out across the land. Other than that, they appeared to enjoy an existence of nonstop eating! No wonder they looked so stout and solid.

Until a few years ago, the main building had been a working blacksmith's forge. The workshop had not changed in centuries – probably not since the last stone was laid! The dominant feature was the raised waist high fire. Based on a pedestal of cut stone, this freestanding piece stood in the middle of the workshop, where it occupied pride of place.

Firedogs guarded the front, and overhead loomed a vast dust-encrusted metal fire hood. From it, an array of smith's tools, files, tongs, and hand wrought chains were hanging. This funnel shaped canopy enticed swirls of salty smelling smoke and stray embers upwards and into its chimney. The flat-topped stone slabs, surrounding the fire bed, housed small leather hand bellows, pokers, and an assortment of wire brushes.

It was the heart and soul of the place.

The heat generated from the sizeable fire came from a mixture of coal and logs. Peat was piled into giant wicker baskets either side of the stone plinth, and left to dry. The peat was mainly used to dampen the fire when leaving it unattended.

The fireside was a fantastically welcome sight when one came in wet through and cold. The stone ledges surrounding the fire were ideal to dry soggy half-chaps, gloves et al. and served to keep mugs of tea hot!

Horse blankets were laid out to dry close by the fire. These, combined with the rich aroma from the peat, produced a double act of evocative smells, which lingered in the air and penetrated your clothing.

It was a scene untouched by time, and full of sensory delights!

Most of the riding equipment was kept in the tack room opposite, with the notable exception of one side-saddle, and a set of saddle bags used to strap across a pony's back to collect and carry grouse. Both these relics were still utilised on occasion.

The slabs that formed the flagstone floor were uneven, cracked, and broken with age, their surface worn smooth by centuries of riding boots. For me, the pièce de résistance was to be found high above, amongst the rafters. They were festooned with cobwebs. Draped in intricate patterns, and of the darkest grey imaginable; shot through with soot.

It was the dirt of ages.

It would be true to say the place was all about atmosphere. A Hollywood film director on finding the venue could justifiably be entitled to exclaim "El Dorado!"

Strange to relate, I was not riding as I was nursing several cracked ribs. So I was awaiting the return of 'the man in my life', quite alone.

He would be, doubtless, appreciating the low levels of natural light available in early December. The pale rays of the winter sun casting subtle shades on the dark green livery of the forest conifers. All to be witnessed, from the best vantage point possible – horseback.

All was unusually still; a dank, cold mid-afternoon in winter. Not a breath of wind, and too early for a frost, which was no doubt already planning a visit!

I was surprised the riders had not returned by now, as it was completely dark. I opened the smithy's door to listen for signs of their approach, but to no avail. As I did so, the inside light shone directly onto the courtyard cobble stones, which were glistening with moisture. The silence was uncanny. Otherworldly.

The night was cloudless, and the rising moon glinted off the damp slates of the roof opposite. Plainly, it would prove a first class hunting night for owls. I turned and purposefully pressed the latch on the outside door firmly with my thumb.

Shut fast.

Returning to warm my hands by the fire, I noted it had now burned down. What remained was a compelling glow from the embers, which drew my eye into the very centre of the intense orange core. It proved an irresistible force. I stared mesmerised into the concentration of colour and heat. My back towards the door.

Having been lured and absorbed, by staring into the light and heat of the fire, I had lost track of time.

I was immersed, yet supremely conscious of my surroundings. A solitary figure, warming its body in an empty building. I stood revelling in this sense of isolation, detached from the outside world; it was as if I was the only person on planet Earth.

The experience verged on the mystical.

Without warning, the door ripped wide open.

Instantly, I pivoted to face…*je ne sais quoi*?

My heart missed several beats, as I was jolted back to reality. The door was swinging noisily on its hinges, with the force of the blast. The docile fire suddenly bust forth, erupting into flames of yellow and orange, and a torrent of sparks catapulted into the air like fireworks.

I tore over to the door. Peering into the darkness, there was no movement, outside all was still, and calm. No wind, no sound. Just a visible dampness. I stood there gazing at the empty yard in darkness.

Terrified, I snapped the door firmly shut, I held my back against the door panels, gasping.

There was nothing to be seen or heard. Silence prevailed.

Yet, somewhere in the far distance, I swear I heard, faintly, the sound of horse's hooves.

Inexplicably, I recalled familiar and enigmatic lines that acted to pacify my senses:

"Ay, they heard his foot on the stirrup,
And the sound of iron on stone,
And how the silence surged softly backward,
When the plunging hoofs were gone."

'The Listeners', 1912, Walter De La Mere.

Sailing through Life

How does an old age pensioner trounce a nation's financial system?

How do you compete in the Sydney to Hobart yacht race all expenses paid?

'Tough nuts to crack', you might assume. Facing the second problem alone I could virtually feel the grey hairs multiplying as I puzzled over the seeming impossible.

My nineteen-year-old son had his heart set on the race for the past three years. He simply could not afford to miss the competition again.

The logistics, the cost of getting there alone, the timeframe, the age factor, and the experience level required. Last but not least, I knew of no one who would be able to help with introductions either in the UK or Australia.

To all intents and purposes, this was a project doomed to failure.

A non-starter in every respect.

Beyond my wildest expectations, I found answers to both these seemingly unrelated questions in one fell swoop on the golf course!

It is worth pointing out that unlike most of my tales, this story did not happen directly to me. It was related by a golf club member, who also acted as the Junior Golf Coordinator (junior members were those under twenty-one years). We walked side-by-side with our trolleys of rattling clubs trundling behind us, and Allister opened the conversation as we approached the first tee.

"Is your boy still keen on sailing? When I drove the juniors' to away matches, he always spoke more about sailing than golf!"

"Probably, because he knew you had a Hobie Cat," I replied.

"He would have been fishing for an invitation I expect," I surmised. "He's had a great season so far, and done well at quite a few regattas. He is a qualified dinghy instructor now. Did you know?"

"Would he like to crew for me on the Sydney to Hobart? I've got an entry this year, and I'm sponsoring a crew."

"Are you serious, Allister? You've got a yacht... But how? It must come at a king's ransom."

"My late wife always said you were nosy, she was right! Come and have a drink in the club after the game and I will reveal all. Everything. Exactly how I came to own a yacht and sponsor an entry in the race privately."

Who could resist this intriguing invitation? My appetite was whetted.

"Better not tell you before the game. I don't want to 'put you off your stroke'," he said with a smile crossing his deeply lined face. I thought I detected a mischievous glint in his eye as I looked up, and replied with gusto, "I shall be all ears at the nineteenth hole!"

We found a secluded and comfortable spot in the clubhouse, overlooking the fairway, and Allister began. In a very matter-of-fact delivery, he explained the background; I could see as he became more intense, interruptions and questions would not be welcome.

He carefully explained how since boyhood he had nursed an ambition to take part in probably the most famous and demanding yacht race in the world – The Sydney to Hobart.

He had been a banker, daily commuting to London, and now he was retired. His oldest friend had been an investment banker and together they had planned, as youngsters, to enter their dream competition from Australia to Tasmania. Old age and family commitments had crept up on them, and they mutually recognised now this would never happen.

Allister had lost his wife recently and his friend was divorced. Without the restraining influence of their women folk, they were up for a challenge. Not a physical challenge, more in the way of a joint business venture. A partnership where they could utilise their extensive experience of the world of business and finance.

Given their offspring were financially buoyant, the two bankers could afford to take a few risks and some 'daring do' was just what they both craved. Financial security would be traded for an exciting knife-edge type of existence. It all seemed desperately out of character. As the story unfolded, my bodily systems were on alert, as I anticipated danger afoot. Perhaps it was because both of them had failed to participate in the great race, they felt undertaking some type of chancy adventure was essential. Before it was too late.

Both men duly sold their properties and cars, cashed in their pensions, and pooled their remaining assets. Apparently, all their worldly wealth was amassed together. They needed the money available to set up their fledgling business, with no costly loans. Thus, their combined wealth was transferred across the Atlantic into the American money market. Part was just earning interest to pay for their rented flat and living costs. The vast majority was to be invested in the S&P 500 index of large cap US equities. This strategy would be employed until the business was operational. They expected to launch the company within two to three months. That would give plenty of time for all the formalities to be completed before the end of the year. After all, it was only September.

To start the ball rolling, instructions were given for the transfer of funds overseas to take place right away.

That evening the two friends celebrated their new entrepreneurial lifestyle by opening a very special bottle of port. The toast was to their new enterprise and partnership, inaugurated September 2001.

The following day, Tuesday 11th, September, an outrage took place that represented a threat to both democracy and world peace. The US money markets would not just be in a spin, or spiralling down, financial collapse, Armageddon, looked a likely consequence across the Atlantic. Anticipating market chaos, panic selling, and with it a disastrous loss of value, in the wake of the terrorist attacks, the New York Stock

Exchange closed. It remained closed until the 17th of September.

This farrago spelled out financial ruin for Allister and his partner. After all, they had managed to break one of the key rules of investment – 'Never put all your eggs in one basket'.

Allister heard the shattering information on the radio with incredulity. His partner collapsed with a heart attack on receipt of the devastating news. This left Allister losing a lifelong friend, a business partner, and all their combined wealth in just 24 hours.

I felt I had to interrupt at this point. However, I really could not think of a single thing to say.

"What on earth did you do then," I managed eventually.

"I went down to Cornwall to stay with my sister in her cottage," he replied. "I had to borrow the money for the train fare. I had no car," he added with feeling.

"What then?" I questioned.

"I just stayed there," he continued. "In retreat."

"All the money would have been invested the day before the crash, at market value – there would be no point in returning to find a letter at the flat confirming my financial ruin." There was a pause while he pulled himself together and resumed his narrative, "When I did go back there was a letter waiting for me, addressed to myself and partner." He confirmed slowly. I looked up encouraging him to continue.

"When I opened it my hands were trembling. I was trying to steel myself up for the inevitable coup de grâce."

At this juncture, he paused and his expression took on a reflective look.

"Actually it was quite good news," he said in an entirely different tone.

"What do you mean?" I asked perplexed.

"What on earth did it say?"

"It was an apology from the broker in New York," he added. "It explained due to a technical hitch how the order had not been executed on Monday the 10th of September 2001 as instructed. However, the deals were all placed as soon as practical after Wall Street reopened on the 17th of September."

"So everything was invested at rock bottom prices," I piped up.

"A stroke of luck like that only comes once in a lifetime," he said sagely.

I was stunned into silence.

Some people manage to simply sail through life. Even their mistakes turn out well in the long run.

Speaking for myself, I always end up butter side down on the carpet; I am not one of the fortunate few.

"So what happened with the new business?" I queried.

"Well, I didn't bother with that. I had no partner now, and to be quite honest, I had had my infusion of excitement. Financially, of course it was no longer necessary."

"Did you just keep the money invested in American markets?" I asked.

"Well, yes, actually within a month, all the major indices had regained their pre 9/11 price levels."

He moved on to say with no emotion, "Most of the equities were bought when the Dow Jones was hovering around the 8000 mark."

On the date the story was unravelled to me in the clubhouse, I knew for a fact that the Dow Jones stood at 27,147.

I follow stock market movements daily. It is both a hobby and an economic necessity in my case. I usually manage to keep slightly ahead with my small investment portfolio held in a stocks and shares ISA. In short, I am a small time investor.

News of this magnitude felt like dreamland. There was a pause whilst I let this revelation sink in, before I asked,

"What happens next, Allister?"

"I decided, since the business never got off the ground, to change tack, and have a go at the Sydney to Hobart. After all it has always been my ambition."

"Gosh! Allister, was that wise? It has got to be a young man's sport."

"No, no! Not as a competitor. Not at my age. As a sponsor. I commissioned a yacht and went out to New South Wales for six months to oversee the build. It will be ready well before this season's race. So now, I am actively looking for a good crew. Do you know anyone who is available, and would fit the bill?" he said with a big grin.

"I will give it some thought," I said smilingly. "I am sure I can come up with a name for you!"

We both exchanged a knowing glance. Then he added, "All expenses paid in your case."

"Shangri-La!" I said out loud.

Astonishing what you can learn through a round of golf!

A pensioner, who unwittingly, gives the entire US financial system a spanking, to become a multi-millionaire. Thus, he is enabled to make his life-long dream, a yacht race, a reality for others.

This has to be worthy of a story. It provides a great example of perceived bad luck and an impossible situation, coming up trumps. A tonic for us all.

But my story is not quite ended...

Allister had been through some choppy waters. He deserved a spell of plain sailing.

Later that month, he was invited as a guest to join a small cruiser visiting the Whitsunday Islands. Just before boarding, he managed to fall and break his leg. He felt obliged to cancel the week-long trip and he remained in Australia for a few more weeks. On recovery, he booked a cruise liner around the Coral Sea, and attended a singles night. There he met a lady, who has since become his wife. He continues to sail through life. In fact, he has never been happier.

Shopaholic

This offering is less of a story, more of a snapshot observation. It appeals, unconditionally, to my sense of humour. After sharing it with the reader, I trust he or she will feel likewise.

The majority of us who inhabit the western world are familiar with the concept of shopping. The basic premise is that an exchange of money, in its various forms and guises, are traded for goods and services required. Thus, a buyer and a seller are necessary for transactions. For those not familiar with the process, put in its simplest form, money changes hands for goods.

So well used and refined is this system, it has virtually replaced its predecessor, trade via barter.

In essence, at least, most people seem to readily get the hang of it.

Although some, it would seem, take just that little bit longer.

Household shopping is at best tedious. It empties the wallet with unparalleled efficiency. In my particular case – at 7:30 am. (store opening time), every Saturday morning, with regular monotony.

Here, at the supermarket, one can be swiftly relieved of hard won cash in return for the dubious benefits of disinfectant, dental floss, and detergent. Then, in the privacy of one's own home, your purchases can be unwrapped, fondled, and relished throughout the forthcoming week.

The key to enduring this wholly necessary, but hapless process is to arrive at the earliest opportunity, when the store is quiet and tolerable. My advice is to conclude the ordeal with a well-earned croissant at the in-store café. This motivating pastry has the double function of providing sustenance, and a goal to see you through the operation!

My experienced buyer's eye alighted on a novice shopper, teetering on the brink of his debut visit. The gentleman was in his mid-seventies, dressed in a tweed sports jacket and crimson corduroy trousers, standing tall and upright, his hand resting on a trolley. He displayed the same self-conscious manner with which men push a pram. The giveaway clue that the poor chap was indeed on the nursery slopes for the first time was that he was holding his purchase above the wire mesh trolley. Strange to relate as it is designed to contain the customer's purchases!

He brandished a small potted plant, which displayed a drooping and dejected single bloom. It looked like a variety of daisy. The petals were a hideous shade of mustard yellow, and it was contained in an equally hideous pumpkin coloured ceramic pot.

I smiled as I passed by.

He returned my friendly gesture by way of an explanation. Apparently, his wife had asked him to buy a plant whilst she waited in the car.

He now appeared to be at a loss. Stranded.

Soon he was straying in the direction of the Fine Wine section of the store. He took up a position on the fringe of the area where he began to 'loiter with intent' and his meandering was taking him into dangerous territory. For a newcomer to the scene, a veritable minefield of temptation awaited him. Could he resist?

He headed straight towards the champagne. Now he had been let off the leash, there was nothing to stop him. Would he succumb?

I watched with interest as the drama unfolded. Once spotted, he moved as if in a trance, towards a particular bottle, which quite obviously held an unmistakable allure.

He possessed the delicate hands of a musician, and his long pliable fingers edged ever closer to the target.

"My favourite!" he exclaimed to the world in general. He cradled the bottle in his pristine hands (I observed en passant, judging by his nails and fingers that he was no gardener.)

His pale and dextrous digits drifted appreciatively across the label. Treasure indeed!

Placing the bottle reverently in the trolley, his hand began to hover over other identical bottles on the shelf. He took five more. Laying them side by side with great care and precision, he seemed to be abandoning the real world in favour of some other more celestial habitat.

I drew closer saying, "What a treat. Are they a present?" He looked mildly horrified at the suggestion, so I innocently remarked as a diversion, "There is an offer on wine and champagne this week. That's why I am buying six bottles of wine." Without a word, he adroitly reached for another half dozen bottles!

I left him in Elysium within the luxury drinks department.

Value for money is what all shoppers seek. It is also true that a bargain is only a bargain if the buyer needs the article in the first place. I felt this sound advice would probably not have been welcome news to the beginner's ears. So I kept it to myself.

Keenly anticipating my breakfast in the café, I made my way firstly towards the checkout. I began to decant my newspaper, six bottles, and a packet of reduced sausages onto the belt. Cautiously wheeling his precious cargo, and making glacial progress towards the till, was the new recruit. He followed behind me to watch and learn from my actions.

The till operator rang up £2.49 for the dead daisy, as his hand struggled into his trouser pocket and eventually produced £2.50. He awaited his change.

It was then he lugged the trolley from behind him, like a child dragging a toy on a string. He seemed distracted, and was exhibiting no real cognisance of actually paying for the champagne.

I knew the bill for twelve bottles would be monumental. My guess was he had no idea of the potential cost. I waited to see what would follow. How would he react?

Could he measure up to the task? Bearing in mind he had only come into the shop for an anticipated spend of two to three pounds on a house plant, by my calculation, he had to be facing an initial bill of five hundred and sixty-four pounds (before discount). Even with the offer price applied, it remained an amazing amount to spend on an unscheduled purchase. An impulse buy!

A pang of guilt for the part I had unwittingly played in his extravagance was beginning to beset me.

Delving into his pocket again, he mumbled, "Ah! I don't seem to have that amount of money." Which was hardly surprising.

The assistant on the till tactfully suggested the use of a card. He managed to produce an array of cards, which his nimble fingers spread before her, not unlike a croupier in a casino, saying: "Pick a card. Anyone will do."

I hoped his luck was in.

"This is the sort of card you had in mind?" he queried earnestly. It was as if he had never used a plastic card up until now.

I continued to observe, fascinated how anyone could spend so much money on a whim, and a consumable whim at that! Let's face it, most people go on holiday for this level of expenditure.

Meanwhile, I amused myself by envisaging the scene in the carpark when he returned to his spouse. Soon my feeling of guilt was displaced and gave way to unbridled mirth. In fact, I laughed all the way to the café. Tackling my much-anticipated classic breakfast pastry, I mused on how the story might have developed.

I was never quite able to decide how the incident ended. The possibilities were:

His wife murdered him.

He met his maker sooner than expected, but with a terrific smile on his face.

The bottles were a Christmas donation to Alcoholics Anonymous.

Of course, I will never know the answer.

I reflected that, occasionally, not knowing the eventual outcome of an episode affords more speculative humour and latent amusement, than knowing the real result!

Apart from value for money on the wine offer, I had gained priceless and long-term entertainment value from my shopping sortie.

More than I had bargained for!

There was no disputing the fact this was one shopping spree where for once, I did have my money's worth!

Bon Marché.

Quid Pro Quo

The farmhouse and steading hid in an isolated hollow deep within the Kielder Forest. The pine trees, close-packed along one side of the track, gave way to a clearing where they lived. Shortly, before the farm entrance, the river crossed the access track where a small stone bridge spanned the water. In this enclave, three quarters of a mile from the nearest road, Rab and Cath Armstrong had worked the land for all their married life. It was where their two boys, now both foresters, had been raised. It was the perfect place for a safe and carefree childhood.

Freshness was the word that sprang to mind and epitomised the scene. Still, fresh air laden with the scent of pine, fresh clear river water and the freshest of green pastureland surrounded their home. It was a lush oasis.

Surprisingly, for an upland farm there was not a sheep to be seen. Rab's herd of beef cattle were largely Aberdeen Angus, and although not many in number, they made up for it in pedigree.

Early morning
At six am sharp, Rab began his daily routine. He dressed in a green all-in-one suit and flat cap, as usual, and walked out to count and check his stock. An early morning mist was secreted into the valley where it hung listlessly. He stamped his feet to ward off the damp cold, as he ventured towards the nearest gate. The silver patina on the gatepost was beginning to melt and form droplets as the sun rose; vanishing the evidence of the touch of overnight frost.

Autumn had made a comeback.

Puffing on his pipe, he advanced into the field to inspect his pride and joy – soon they would be expecting supplementary feed, and later they would be overwintering in the cattle court nearer the house.

His attention was distracted momentarily by a small piece of paper lying in the furrow made by a tractor tyre. It was a fifty-pound note. Stiffly, he bent down to examine the item, as he picked it up out of the mud, he noticed it was not alone, there were two more notes lying close by. Straightening up, he gazed about in consternation. Were there more to be found?

It was then he caught sight of a flattened patch in the ferns, as if deer had been resting overnight. Moving closer he saw a large black sports holdall. Just as he was thinking *'damn picknickers leaving their rubbish...'*, the penny dropped. It was then he made the connection. Edging closer he grabbed the handles and cautiously unzipped the bag.

What a revelation!

It was crammed to capacity with brown high denomination sterling banknotes. Temporarily ignoring the bullocks, he hurried straight home. Several times, he stopped, in case this experience was a chimera, and just felt into the bag for confirmation. It was money all right, and right down to the bottom of the bag!

Rab had never been a gambling man. He not even once had taken part in the lottery! But, this he determined, was one chance he was going to take. Without reservation for the first time in his life, he decided to take a gamble.

Mechanically, his feet moved him homeward; his mind was elsewhere and abuzz.

Who would be the rightful or legal owner of the treasure-trove?

Would it be the Forestry Commission? After all, they owned the farm and its land.

Would it be the Crown?

One piece of unavoidable logic was the fact that the stash was not his. It should not therefore be in his possession!

It was a risk that he was prepared to take.

Plans were already formulating in his head. First and foremost, a trip to the Perth bull sales – an absolute 'must' to improve the stock. Second, his coveted ambition to export cattle semen for use in Artificial Insemination (AI) breeding programs abroad could then be launched. That would really put the farm on the map, and expand the business no end.

Something for Cath, a new car was much overdue. Also, to realise her dream of glamping at the farm. They could now afford to buy the yurts required to upgrade and compliment the farmhouse bed and breakfast.

As his thoughts extended and progressed along these lines, he began wondering if a trip to Australia for the marketing of the AI project could be tax deductible…and part holiday too… The possibilities were alluring and endless.

Arriving at his backdoor, these flights of fantasy were suddenly brought down to earth. He had qualms on two counts.

Had he abandoned his moral compass?

What if Cath would have none of it?

I adored the Armstrongs. Whenever I was in the vicinity of Kielder Water or Kielder Forest, I found an excuse to visit and stay. I was equally drawn to the place itself. It possessed a rare and serene atmosphere. I found it compelling. To me it was a magnet.

Rab kept a well-ordered farm. Cath very competently managed the house, its neat walled garden and the B & B business. The farm was a perfectly secluded hideaway 'off the beaten track' where tourists could enjoy first rate birdwatching and walking in the adjacent forest.

The couple had an enviable relationship, crowned with a contented unfussy lifestyle; they seemed to blend into the landscape. Rab and Cath were well matched they made a good team.

Cath was always busy. Practical in every aspect of her life. She was creative with her hands and was a prominent member of the nearest Woman's Rural Institute (WRI). She baked for the WRI, took part in their flower arranging, knitting and photographic activities. A plain, but good cook, everything from jam to wine was concocted in her kitchen. The Aga was her byword for pleasure.

A good solid dress size 14, she was an attractive soul with strong curly black hair, and a cheery personality. She was full of life and energy. It had been her enterprising idea to have a small extension to the farm, catering for bed and breakfast. This was her forte, as she could work from home, and over the summer months, bring in a steady source of revenue. She enjoyed the contact with people, largely heading to and from Scotland, and the extra cooking necessitated by their visits. This added income was used to upgrade the house and its interior. Lately, she had taken to investing in a few bygones and antiques for her household, and was particularly proud of her recently acquired mahogany roll top desk. In summary, she was an archetypal 'home maker', and as such made an ideal farmer's wife.

Her gumboots were always found at the back door, (water hose beside them for quick cleaning). Ready and waiting should she be required to nip out, and help move some livestock at short notice. Rab was indeed a fortunate man.

The farmer, several years her senior, was the ultimate 'Steady Eddie', he was not the sort to make sparks fly. He was kind, gentle, and taciturn. He exhibited a very measured approach to life, and had an aura of controlled strength. It took a great deal of time to get to know him; there was more to him than met the eye. He also exhibited, on a strictly limited basis a good sense of fun.

A fine example of his humorous side was revealed in a story he related to me, which he obviously enjoyed immensely.

How the chef at the local pub, suspecting a gas leak from one of the gas cylinders stored in the cellar, went to investigate. Unable to find the light switch, he struck a match. The resulting explosion had blown up the entire pub and its contents to smithereens. Only the facade wall was left standing! This had brought a slow smile to Rab's lips as the story had clearly appealed to him. He then had added how the stuffed fox, formerly housed in a glass case (besides which I had enjoyed many bar dinners), was blown high into the tallest tree in the car park where it had lodged. Apparently, to date, no one had been able to get it down!

This tale had caused a most infectious wave of laughter throughout the household and throughout Northumberland to the border.

Rab's hobby was collecting obsolete military equipment – largely from the Second World War. He had a barn full of motorcycles, Bren guns, parts of tanks and other military hardware. When not engaged with restoring these items, he would, on occasion, visit the pub. The latter activity, however, was now rendered somewhat historical.

Mid-Day

It was clear that Rab had already taken the decision to keep the money, without consultation with Cath *How could she object?* he reasoned.

He was just about to find out!

Calmly, Rab explained it all to his wife.

She took on an expression of bewilderment, akin to a Japanese sumo wrestler at a weight watchers class. Her eyes opened ever wider in utter amazement.

'Manna from Heaven' – was all she said.

Relieved by her non-judgemental stance, and her perception of the windfall as a 'godsend', Rab outlined the next step.

Over lunch, their main meal of the day, they agreed to hold the money in the house under lock and key in the newly acquired roll top desk. No attention grabbing purchases would be made in the short term. However, Rab eagerly rang to find out the dates of the next Perthshire livestock sale. They then decided to drive over to Hexham at the weekend to book the trip to Australia and pay the deposit in cash.

After the meal, Rab went towards the machinery barn and took out his welding kit; he went about his work as if nothing had happened. It was business as usual.

Cath called out across the yard: "Don't forget to drive up to the main road and take down the B & B sign today, will you?" She doubted he heard her.

Returning to clear away the dishes, Cath then piled the mountain of ironed linen on top of the Aga lids. She also resumed the normal rhythms of her life, and began by reaching for her knitting wool and pattern. Only to be interrupted by the loud and discordant jangling of the extension phone. Cath took the call. It was a couple who wanted B & B for the night. She explained they were about to close for the winter, but the person at the other end of the line sounded desperate, and she acquiesced. Instantly, she regretted her decision.

Secretly, she was rather looking forward to the end of the season; it was hard work, with no domestic help, and having their home back solely for family use was something she had been longing to realise.

She let out her characteristic long and meaningful sigh 'eeeh!'

***

Affable, mercurial, and gullible was how Cath viewed her younger sister, Jackie. It would be fair to say that the notion of 'saving for a rainy day' did not feature in Jackie's psyche. A lifetime's dedication to the pursuit of a bargain, particularly in the realm of fashion, had resulted in her ill-assorted and often ill-advised wardrobe.

She numbered among the rare breed who were proud possessors of not one, but two pairs of pink suede boots. Jackie's wardrobe was the principle reason she was constantly skint, which made her something of a pest.

Conversely, Cath only bought what she needed, and wore it. Even if it turned out to be a wardrobe mistake!

Jackie's other weakness was competitions. Cath's sister was obsessed with competitions. She entered everything she could find – even if she didn't want the prize! Cath always considered this 'hobby' a complete waste of time. Jackie ensured all her friends snipped out coupons from various products and sent them to her, so she could try her luck. Competitions had become similar to compulsive gambling for her younger sister.

Ironically, whilst Cath was peering out of the kitchen window facing the bird feeder, her eye glimpsed a packet lying on the sill. It was promoting a competition. The first prize was a vehicle, plus a contribution towards a new business idea, which would diversify the work you currently perform. She read on with interest.

Instead of sending the item to her sister, as usual, she decided to complete the pro forma herself. Perhaps she could now win a car, and achieve her dream of providing glamping in yurts at the farm without using their windfall. Well, she reasoned the wheel of fortune was in their direction. Why not? The entry was postage paid, which sealed her decision to take part and have a go.

Her lips curled into a smile as she thought of Jackie.

The competition her sister would dearly love to have won was the first prize of a £5000 shopping spree in Harrods sponsored by a fruit company. She had won. But not the first prize. Her reward was a boxed set of apple shaped cufflinks!

The only other success she had met with, despite years of competing, was winning a case of bubble gum. Fearing for her dentures, she gave her trophy away as a raffle prize – she couldn't find anyone who would accept it as a gift!

Later the Same Day

It was during the afternoon when the delivery postman arrived. Cath passed the postie a few items of farm correspondence to take, and received a bundle of junk mail in return. She also handed him her competition entry. The closing date was tomorrow, so she crossed her fingers it would arrive on time.

Later in the afternoon, a single knock on the door revealed her expected guests. A scruffy looking man and a shabbily dressed woman had arrived at the farmhouse door. Cath took an instant dislike to the pair.

She escorted them to their room, and was suspicious when they appeared to have no luggage. Just a plastic carrier bag between them. The male had a pale thin anaemic face, with weasel-like features, and a Glasgow accent. The woman wore a hat, which largely obscured her face. She did not speak.

They paid upfront and said they did not want breakfast in the morning.

Prior to shutting the house down for the night, as Cath was watering her indoor plants, she reiterated to Rab her misgivings regarding the paying guests. Her hackles were up, and she would be pleased when they left. Wearily, he dismissed her concerns and told her to focus on their newfound wealth. She should be happy, and he promised a little celebration on Saturday evening to console her.

Before turning in, Cath hesitated, standing on the rag rug outside the occupied guest bedroom. Not a sound from within. This seemed to deepen her sense of unease. She was absolutely certain something was wrong. But what?

The Following Day

After a restless night, she came down to the kitchen, which was in darkness. Rab had the yard lights on and was already outside smiling reassuringly through the window at her. He went round to the front of the house to see off their guests, but he had just missed them as their van was already travelling over the stone bridge.

Having made tea, Cath turned on the radio. A piece on the local radio caught her attention. She dived to turn up the volume, but alas, it was too late, the newscast had moved on. She would have to wait another half hour for the next newscast.

Instinctively, she rushed into the parlour. A ghastly sight greeted her eyes. The room had been ransacked, paper and documents were strewn everywhere. The roll top desk had been savagely smashed open. The bag containing the cash had gone. She screamed for Rab.

Together they sat in the kitchen, Rab tightly holding her hand. Cath never cried, but for once, he heard her whimper. Husband and wife listened together and heard a re-run of the news. Without a doubt, they were in an unenviable position. There followed a police appeal to 'help with their enquiries'.

A break out from Durham jail of a male inmate, aided by a female from outside, had taken place yesterday and the pair were on the run. It was thought they would be headed for

Scotland. A brief description of the couple was given, and the public were warned against approaching the duo. He had been serving a sentence for armed robbery.

The unspoken question was how could they help recapture the criminals without disclosing the cash they had kept?

Summoning all her pragmatism, Cath took the lead by saying: "I think we should let sleeping dogs lie."

Rab concluded the conversation by adding, "The police are bound to catch them."

Finally, after some thought, he said, "Well, I suppose we are no better off, and no worse off than we were before. We have only lost what wasn't ours in the first place!"

Of course, his last comments were correct. They each managed to force a weak smile.

Sitting and reflecting in the quietness, with only the familiar ticking of the parliament clock in the background, they jumped when the phone bell rang, which broke the spell they seem to have been under. Rab willingly bounced into action in an effort to break the strange melancholy that engulfed them both.

He returned to say the call was for Cath, it was the PR department of some company, he had not heard the name. He said it didn't sound like a sales call.

Cath took the phone from him, without thinking, she was still experiencing symptoms of shock. Unexpectedly, her face visibly brightened as she listened to the caller. Rab heard her say: "Thank you. Thank you so much," with obvious gratitude.

"What was all that about?" he enquired, as Cath plonked down heavily on the chair, grinning from ear to ear. Rab waited for her response patiently.

Turning towards him, she said, "Eeh! I can't wait to see Jackie's face."

"What are you talking about woman?"

"Whatever next?" she asked aloud.

"I've just won a competition prize," she boasted.

"Cufflinks or bubble-gum?" he asked.

"Howay!" she responded, and just to add drama to the situation, she paused before concluding, "No. Not quite. It's a Land Rover and cheque for four yurts."